D0252351

JEREMY
STONE

JEREMY STONE

Lesley Choyce

Red Deer Press

Copyright © 2013 Lesley Choyce
5 4 3 2 1
All rights reserved. No part of this publication may be reproduced, stored in a retrieval system or transmitted, in any form or by any means, without the prior written permission of Red Deer Press or, in the case of photocopying or other reprographic copying, a licence from Access Copyright (Canadian Copyright Licensing Agency), 1 Yonge Street, Suite 800, Toronto, ON, M5E 1E5, fax (416) 868-1621.

Published in Canada by Red Deer Press
195 Allstate Parkway, Markham
ON, L3R 4T8
www.reddeerpress.com

Published in the U.S. by Red Deer Press
311 Washington Street, Brighton,
Massachusetts 02135

Edited for the Press by Peter Carver
Cover image courtesy of iStockphoto
Text and cover design by Daniel Choi

We acknowledge with thanks the Canada Council for the Arts, and the Ontario Arts Council for their support of our publishing program. We acknowledge the financial support of the Government of Canada through the Canada Book Fund (CBF) for our publishing activities.

Library and Archives Canada Cataloguing in Publication
Choyce, Lesley, 1951-, author
    Jeremy Stone / Lesley Choyce.
ISBN 978-0-88995-504-2 (pbk.)
    I. Title.
PS8555.H668J47 2013   jC813'.54   C2013-904217-2
Publisher Cataloging-in-Publication Data (U.S.)
Choyce, Lesley.
    Jeremy Stone / Lesley Choyce.
[184] p. : cm.
Summary: Jeremy Stone is a First Nations teenager trying to find out where he fits in the world, particularly as a loner in a new high school. In this contemporary free verse novel, Jeremy is guided by voices from the spirit world, especially that of his grandfather, Old Man, as he explores a new relationship with the intense Caitlan, deals with the school bully, and tries to keep his family together.
ISBN: 978-0-88995-504-2 (pbk.)
1. Bullying – Juvenile fiction. 2. Racism – Juvenile fiction. I. Title.
[Fic] dc23   PZ7.C569je   2013

Printed and bound in Canada by Kromar Printing

Dedicated to the memory of Rita Joe

When I Learned to Talk Again

The first words were
                          leave me alone.
Said it like I meant it
to that person

                                     some idiot

who examined me.
My mom was determined I should go

                                     back to school.
Think about it.

                                          School.

Yeah, as soon as I told the shrink or
          whatever, whoever that pisser was,
to kiss my ass (guess I said that too)
he said, then my mom said, and the school said
I was ready

                          to go back to school.

Let Me Take You Back First

Shut up.
Just shut up.
Everyone
                kept saying it to me.
                                      Shut
the hell
                up.
So I
did.

And I fell in love with silence.
        Head
        over
        heels.
The words just stopped flowing,
stopped jumping
                                out of my
                                    mouth.

The great god of silence took me on
as a disciple.
I found a new wilderness
inside me.

A beautiful place
to camp,
place to hang out with spirits
place to live alone with just

me.

Jeremy Stone, Me

No, don't stone me.
Me, Stone.
Like a rock.
You know, you can throw me but
you can't break me

                              or crack me open

                                             easily.

I'm that hard.
Stone hard.
Stoner, some said.

                          Well, yeah, maybe sometimes
but not often.
Stoney stuck, though
as a nickname
sometimes.

I am (or was, not sure) a sink-to-the-bottom
stone,
language heavy inside me
but not always getting out to breathe.
Had this hard outer shell—

                          plain-looking, I know, gray, dull.
But inside.
Yes, inside.

All hard jagged crystal.
Beautiful in sunlight but if kept in the dark,
damn
just a little too weird.

To get me
                                to understand me,

you have to know what
a geode
               is.
My father
                    gave me one
this gray nothing-looking rock
when I was little.
Break it open, he said.
But I couldn't.

                             So he did

and inside
               it was all hollow
                    with tiny glittering crystals.
Pointed, shiny.
God, look at that
                   my father said.

Gotta love that rock.

Oh Yeah, My Father

My missing father
going

            going

                        gone.

I was ten and he kept getting
      older

            thinner

                  farther

                       away.

Did I tell you that my people,
his people,
      go back 10,000 years here?
Maybe more. Who knows?
Maybe my ancestors were flint and obsidian and coal and
                           amethyst.

We go back to the Stone Age.
Hah.
            Get it.
My father's humor.
He had humor once when he had a big belly

but
he
thinned
down.

                                        He lost

a lot of things.
I saw the lights going out
                in his eyes
as he
got more hollow
more hurt.

So he shared that hurt sometimes.
                        No humor in that. Nope.
He shared it by hitting me.
He hit me some.
                        Not too much.
(It's okay, Dad. I forgive you.)
He stopped hitting
when he
                                        disappeared.

I missed him right away.
Better to be hit
than to not have him at all.

                        Damn.

I Had a Grandfather Once

I really
            did
and he was filled with history
        fed up with history, too
                    but he told stories of the old times
before
                                you know.
He said his grandfather had handed all those stories
over to him.
When my grandfather wasn't telling old-time stories
he was kinda quiet.
People made fun of him
        when he went outside the community:
                the long hair
                the way he walked
                the hesitation in his speech.
His stories were great
        but he couldn't shed the dark part of that damn history
and I don't think he was good with understanding time.
He told me this:
        One day our people are happy as clams
        and hunting saber-toothed tigers and big hairy
        mastodons.
                The next thing you know

                        the Europeans
show up
                        and the fun is all over.

Everyone just called him Old Man
so I did too.

My Grandfather's School

Old Man had gone to one of those places,
                  a residential school,
where you dressed like everyone else, slept in big rooms with
everyone else,
ate the same food as everyone else, spoke English like
everyone else, got
punished like everyone else.
The cops brought you back if you tried to run away
and be yourself. Be different.
And if you got sick and threw up at mealtime
                        they made you eat
                              your own puke.

It's called education,
        Old Man said.
So you run away again
and they bring you back
                  so they can teach you
                  how to stop being
                        who you are
and learn to be

                        someone else.

Who I Am

At my new school,
at first
no one really knows who I am.
They think maybe I am Italian
or from South America.
No one knows me here   not even me.
But I think I am becoming more like my grandfather.
Old Man.

                                  I remember his stories

but not much about my own past.
So I need to find little Jeremy Stone.
I'm pretty sure he was never Italian.

My mother promised to help me find him.
                             Find me.
                                 She'd been trying
to tug some words out of me for three years.
Before that she had lectured me for being
          too loud
          too rude
          too curious.
And then she really lost it
and hit me. (Like my dad had done, only different.)
                    At least I think she hit me

or someone did anyway.

That's when I stopped talking.
Went silent like a stone.

But I'm not gonna blame her
No.
Not my mother. She tried her best
but had wrestling matches with her own personal demons.
Ya know.
Drink.
Men (after my father evaporated).
Some kind of pills.
She said none of it would kill her.
Not even the men,
or the smokes. (Tobacco is sacred, she said.)
Changed her mind after the coughs.

Good thing too.
Me,
I never smoked.

Not tobacco anyway.
But my mom
she loved me
and thanked me when I found my tongue again
and words spilled out. But I only spoke to people who
really knew who I was
and that was

a pretty small group.

The New Kid

That's me.
Like I said,
I'm fairly new at this school
                and don't say much
                'cause
                        it's easier to hide that way.
I guess word finally got out
        on where I came from, who my parents were
so they started calling me
                the Indian
since I am the only one in school
although some call me
the hermit.   And there are other names.
                               Cruel names.
Here's what the Indian does at school:
        he keeps to himself,
        he doesn't give eye contact,
        he drops his books a lot,   and
        he's afraid to look at girls.
They say maybe he's on drugs
this Indian Jeremy Hermit Stone.
He's somewhere, man,
                but he's not here.

The teachers say:

>at least he's polite,
>
>he's not much trouble,
>
>he always sits in the same seat,
>
>he's shy,
>
>he's doesn't talk or text on a cell phone,
>
>and he looks awfully sad.

One of them, Mr. Godwin, asks

>Jeremy, are you there?

I say

No,

not really.

Hope

I'm hoping,
(yeah, I do that sometimes)

                                         I hope

that some   not so distant   day
I will feel like a normal
person.

                                 Don't know when

or how.
But someday.

I
was
at
the water fountain the other day
and pretended I
was in   the forest
                                                   drinking clear water
                                                   from
                                                   a
                                                   mountain
                                                   stream.

When I looked up   there was
a girl
looking right at me.

I said, I'm sorry,
'cause I thought I was in her way
and maybe she was
thirsty.
Then I stood back
but kept my thumb
on the button.
I offered her
the stream
and the forest
and the mountain too.

Walking

I think the girl smiled.
                    Maybe she did,
or maybe I imagined it.
And then I got scared
                    and had to walk
                                        away.

Walking was more my thing:
walking away from,
walking into,
walking out of.
I could walk until there was no more of me left.
Into the woods,   along the creek bed.
I was never alone.
There was almost always my companion.
                    My grandfather.
                    Old Man would be there
even though he's been dead and gone for a long while,
this very important someone from the past.
He didn't actually speak but there was this:
          sometimes I could hear his thoughts in my head.

He'd tell me,   This is what you do
                    if you want to survive
                    in this ole world.

Don't say too much.
Don't feel too much.
Don't reveal who you are.
Don't stay in one place too long.

The trees are there for you if you need them
and the birds.
Always trust the sky.
The wind will tell you what you need to know.
And the stars.
But don't stare at the sun.
Or you'll go blind.

Sitting Still Through Math Class is Hard

It was math   and all about numbers
but it didn't seem to add up to anything.
Zero + zero x zero = zero.
The teacher, Mr. Diamond,
knew I was a long-lost stone and didn't usually call on me.
If he asked me, though,
if he asked me for an answer to anything,
I would have just said eleven.
That's what the Old Man had told me to say
if someone asked me a question I couldn't answer.
He never explained why, though.

                Some of the other kids
                stared at me
                and I tried not to notice.
      I tried very hard
not to notice
but when Diamond started talking to the equation on the
blackboard
somebody   flicked   a paper clip   at me.
                        Hit me on the cheek.
                        Fuck.

I looked over   at him. The creep.
Shithead. Scumbag.   No, I didn't say it out loud.
Held it inside, instead.

His buddy was laughing
but his laughing sounded more like hiccups.
I studied Diamond's back.   He was now acting like he
was making out with those symbols and numbers on the board.
Adults.   Go figure.

I wanted to run but told my legs
to stay put.
Told my ass
to stay seated.
Told my brain
to think about the trees—
white pines in the wind.
And then Old Man said
Just think about eleven.

                    If it gets real bad
                    say eleven eleven inside your skull.

If it gets real, real bad
I told myself
I'll make myself invisible.

Somewhere in the Back of the Class

Way in the back, she must have been sitting—
                                        the girl.

I couldn't just turn around.
Trees can't do that.
But someone tapped me on the shoulder,
        handed me a note.
Little folded up piece of lined paper
that made no sense at first.   On top it said this:
                                        Loser
                                        Welcome to Hell.
On the back it said:
But when I opened it,
Someone with beautiful handwriting had written:
        Don't let the bastards get to you.

                              And then a name:
                        Caitlan.
The girl had passed the note to me.
The other messages were just a couple of my
warm and fuzzy classmates
Adding their regards.
                        The bastards didn't matter, though.
I finally turned and ignored the sea of ugly faces
and tuned in to her smile.
Would have just kept locked onto that smile too

but Old Man was reminding me
if I kept staring at the sun

well, you know.

When My Father Talked

When my father used to talk to just me and no one else
                              he sometimes talked about
the black dog
but the dog didn't have a name not a dog name
                              anyway.
My mom had to later explain to me
that the black dog
was depression
and it would bite my father hard and deep
and not let go.

So I knew all about the black dog when it came up snarling at
me
three years ago.
There I was
a thirteen-year-old boy just off the reserve
with his own ugly pet dog.
                              He didn't bite
                              at first.

He was skinny and afraid
and needed to be taken care of
but he was the same kind of dog
that my father knew all too well.
                              And when he turned on me

                              there was nothing I could do.

At first I felt the pain, the teeth,
saw the meanness in his eyes.
                              At first I thought,
                              not his fault maybe,
probably couldn't help it   but he hung on
        and after a while it stopped hurting.
                              I think the teeth
injected something into my blood
that made my mind go numb.
                              And I began to like the feeling—
like being dead
but still breathing.

The Girl

What about the girl?
When class was over, she had moved quickly
down
the
aisle
like
the
wind
right
past
me
and
she
was
gone.

Everyone left quickly like there was a fire or something
and I was left there with the teacher.

                Mr. Diamond didn't know what to say to me.
                      Maybe he'd never

spoken to a kid like me before,
someone off the reserve.

                  What was your name?

Jeremy Stone, I said.

That was my name
and still is.
He smiled, I think.
Hard to tell with white people
sometimes   whether they are
                              smiling
or laughing at you   or just awkward and pale like that
but I don't think he was unkind,
just awkward and pale
and good with numbers
but not words
or people.

Getting Lost in the Halls

That's never much fun
for someone like me.
And I didn't ask anyone
where the gym was
so I showed up late
after Old Man finally said to me
                            just follow the smell of stinky socks.
And he was right as usual.

I was new of course and everyone else
knew what was going on.
Pretty weird, really.
Wrestling.
By the rules
but wrestling.   Just like when I was little and
                                        my cousins and me
                                wrestled in the living room
                                until someone got hurt.
It usually wasn't me.   Don't know why.
But now we were paired off
and I ended up with the Paper Clip Creep.
                            Someone said to him
                            Thomas,
        looks like

                              you get to wrestle
                         Geronimo.
Geronimo was me.   (I guess now I had a new name.)
Thomas Heaney was him.
I didn't understand the rules
but no one was explaining.
So he quickly   slammed me on the mat
and that took me back
to the living room.
Only now I was bigger
and Old Man was yelling to me: Get up, Jeremy Stone
                                        and fight like a warrior.

                                   I had forgotten all about
                  the warrior.

                                      Use your enemy's strength,
against him,   said the familiar voice of
                                        Old Man.

I twisted out from under
Paper Clip's armpits
like a snake
and stepped back,
waited for him
to lunge
and miss.   Then I threw myself on him
                                   and knelt on his back
                                        like I was praying.

The gym teacher blew a whistle

and yelled at me to get up.
I got up
and Thomas
glared.
I said   I'm sorry, Paper Clip
but didn't mean it.
Now the others were laughing at him,   not me.
But just then someone farted loudly
and that was the
end
of that.

I had Forgotten about Geronimo

Geronimo was a warrior
I read about in a book.
Old Man didn't like Geronimo
                        but then he hated everything about
                                        the history
            of North America
            after 1492
and the arrival   of you know who.
But I read the book anyway

                            and could see that
if they had just left Geronimo and his people alone
he would
have been peaceful.   But
it didn't work out that way
so
he
fought
back.
Fought
hard.
Fought well.
But that is not what I liked about Geronimo.
They said
he could

walk
without
making
footprints.

He could
see far into the future.
And if he needed to,
he could tell the sun
not to come up
if he needed darkness
for protection.
Geronimo said:

> "I was born on the prairies where the wind blew free
> and there was nothing to break the light of the sun."

In the past,
thinking about Geronimo
sometimes
made the black dog
run away.
And it helped me to pin
Paper Clip that day
although
Old Man wanted to take credit for that.

The Fish in the River

I think I have a problem understanding time.
                         Just like my grandfather.
I slip
into the past
and don't know why.
Old Man says it's because   sometimes
I just have my head up my ass   and he'll say,
                                   how is the view
                                   up there
                                        today?

But that's just because
he thinks it's a bad thing
to spend too much time
in the past.
Anybody's personal past
unless you can go way
way back to the old days
when it was always quiet
in the woods
and you could just reach into any stream
and lift out
a
big fish
to cook for dinner.

I have a hard time
hanging on   to the present.
The present is like that big fish and I am trying to hold onto it
            so I can
                                    cook it for dinner.
But it keeps jumping back into the river
and swimming away
upstream (into the past)
or downstream (into the future).

It's been a very long while
since my father   went to the river
and caught a real fish
and my mother   cooked it
                                 and we ate it

with my cousins.
        That's some fish,
            my mother kept saying.
And my father kept saying,
                                    It was like
                                    that fish
                                    wanted me to
                                    catch him

and feed him to my family.

But my father left the next day
to go look for work   on the oil rigs out West.
And I felt bad
because I didn't eat all my fish,

                    didn't like all the bones.

But I should have saved those bones
to remember my father by.

Even
fish bones
should not
be wasted.

Caitlan Speaks

You need me in your life,
    she said.
      Just like that.   Out of the blue.
You don't want to be alone
in this school
in this life
ever.

Do you know about Jenson Hayes?
    she asked.
        Who is Jenson Hayes?   I asked.
Jenson Hayes was the one person I truly loved.
He was the one.
But I never told him.
And that was stupid of me.
And now he's gone.
You remind me of him.
        I do?

Yes.
Difference is you are here
and Jenson's not.
      Oh shit,   I said.
Oh shit is right,

Caitlan said
and then kissed me hard on the mouth.

The Difference Between Me
and Jenson Hayes

Follow me,   Caitlan said.
She led me to a janitor's closet.
Don't worry about Fred. Fred is cool, she told me.
Fred is the janitor.
Fred lets me chill in the janitor's
closet whenever I need to chill.
          Which was often as it turned out.

          There were two classroom chairs in there.
          We sat.
          She stared at me intently.
You're quieter than Jenson, she said.
Taller and quieter. Darker skin.
But you've got his eyes.
And the deer in the headlights look.
          Yeah, that was me.   I liked this girl, the girl
from the mountain stream
          but she scared me a little.
                    Caitlan, what are we doing in here?
Talking, she said. Getting to know each other.
I know you've got issues, she said.
          You don't have to be a psychic to know that

I guess, I answered.
We've all got issues. I just want to make
sure you don't get fucked over.

                                    What do you mean?
Like Jenson. Fucked over and fucked up.
What happened?

What Happened to Jenson Hayes

He wasn't strong enough
when we were together
cared for him
when I played with his hair

well, sometimes he was
when I told him how much I

when we did other stuff.

     I had to ask.
They got to him.

What happened to Jenson?

          They?

You know. The bastards. The shitheads.
The cruel ugly fucks who think they run the world.
            Oh them, I said,
    pretending I knew who they were.
Thomas Heaney for one. The lout who hit you with a paper clip.
He was the worst.
    I didn't tell her that I had pinned him in wrestling.
    That would have been bragging.
           Paper Clip, I said.
Jenson didn't deserve any of that crap.
But he needed to be stronger.
He was very sensitive.
Look,
here's
a poem
he wrote
for
me.

Jenson's Poem

Sunlight on water
spring
green leaves on all the trees
warm sweet air
birds singing
everywhere.
You beside me
on the green moss
stretched out
our bodies
touching
forever.

Forever

Yes. Forever. That was Jenson.
Sensitive, creative, romantic, idealistic
and easily hurt.   A fatal combination.

       I swallowed hard. Oh, I forgot to tell you,
       we were sitting in those classroom chairs,
       facing each other, Caitlan and me, and our knees
       were touching
       and I was holding Jenson's poem that I just read
       and I was thinking I really loved this girl,
       this weird, hyper, intense, savagely beautiful girl
       with long dark hair (Indian hair, I kept thinking).
       And dark Indian eyes, too. This girl still hung up
       on an old boyfriend
       but that was okay because our knees were touching
       and she had taken me into the
       janitor's closet alone.
       This was so much better than being in class
       but I didn't know what would
       happen after we walked out of that closet
       and back into the real world of school.
       But I didn't have the whole story.

                 What happened to Jenson?
I asked again.   Did he move away?

Did he stop talking to you?
No, she said.
It wasn't like that.
Jenson is dead.

I sometimes think I still hear his voice. Sometimes I think I feel
him touching me on the shoulder.
Sometimes …
I'm sorry if this is uncomfortable for you, she said.
I'm a little intense, I know. It scares people sometimes.

I'm not scared, I said.
But she could feel my knees shaking a little.
I have shaky knees when I get nervous
and sweaty hands.

I shouldn't say this, Caitlan said.

Say what?
Well, you have the look.

What look?
The victim look.

The what?
You have this look that says you've been hurt, you are vulnera-
ble, and if someone wants to get you, to pick on you, to harass
you, to hurt you, they will target you and wear you down. People like Thomas Heaney know that look and will dog you. And
he's not the only one. People like him will find you all through-
out your life.

That's not fair, I said.

I'm stronger than that.

You don't know me.

(No, I didn't actually say that out loud.

I just thought that.)

I swallowed hard again.

Caitlan leaned forward until her forehead was touching mine.

But I won't let that happen to you.

Not this time.

How Jenson Died

It was such a big story for such a small closet,
such a sad story for such an ordinary day,
such a dark and tragic tale from such a beautiful girl.

Caitlan said,
We had been going together for a couple of years. He wrote me
poems. We went on long walks. We never ate meat, never used
cell phones, only bought used clothes, refused to watch television. He taught me to meditate and to breathe properly. We
read long old novels together. He taught me the names of birds
and flowers. We knew for a fact we were living in the wrong
century. The wrong time. The wrong place. But there was not
much of anything we could do about it.
And then we broke up.

                                        Why?

I don't know exactly.
I think everything we did was just
too
intense.

                          I nodded.

It was almost a year ago. We didn't talk for a week. My mom
had often said we were too young to be so serious. His mom
said it too. Maybe that had something to do with it. We were

on a roller-coaster ride. Sometimes we were on top. But then we dropped to the bottom when we let the world get to us ... when it really got to us. When it got to us so badly ... do you understand?

Yes, I said. I understand.

When that happened.
It was bad.

There were black dogs in the room with us now.
Three of them. I could hear them breathing.
I could smell their breath.

While we were not speaking, Thomas and a couple of his friends had been dogging Jenson. And he was weak. I didn't know this at the time. But he had no one to turn to.
And they said something, did something. I don't know what.
He took his own life.
Pills.
Alone in his bedroom.
And there
was nothing
I could do
to bring him
back.

Caitlan Cried

The floodgates opened
and I held her
and then she sobbed
and blew her nose on my sleeve
and said she was
sorry.
I knew it was my job to stay strong right now.
                              That was all I knew.
I silently told the fuckin' black dogs to fuck off
and they did.

                                        And suddenly,
Old Man was in the little closet with us.
        He looked a little older, a little more tired. Bent over.
        I heard him speak in my head in the usual way.
        Oh boy, he said, you sure got your hands full
and he nodded at Caitlan.
I shrugged. You look tired, I said silently to him.
                Yeah, he said. I've been staying up late.
                So much to think about on this side.
                She's pretty, he said.
                But it looks like a bit of trouble.
I must have looked puzzled because he added,
                        It's okay, though. It's always okay.
                Caitlan was pulling herself together

We've been in here a long time. Fred
will probably show up. But that's okay.
It's only Fred and he's cool. But we
should get
to our next class. I'm sorry.

Nothing to be sorry about, I said.

Probably best if we don't
leave here together
in case somebody sees.

Right.   Old Man nodded.

And then she was gone
and I was alone again
with my grandfather.   You like her? he asked.

What's not to like? I answered.

She's got Indian hair,
Indian eyes.

I noticed. That's good.

It's all good, he said.
When you get to where
I am, you get to see things
on a lot of levels.
And your eyes work in different ways.
I get to see the sunset
from the other side of the sun
and the sunrise too.
And people—
you can see people inside out,
if you know what I mean.

What can I do to help her?

You'll need to be careful.

She could drag you down.

But she said she was trying to help *me*.

She's kind. But a bit intense.

You noticed.

I don't miss much.

She needs you. So there's that.

Can't ignore that.

Just don't fall in love.

Oops.

Right.

Sounds like she's still in love with Jenson Hayes.

There's that.

That can't be good.

She didn't have closure.

Everyone needs that.

What can I do about that?

Old Man straightened his back. That's what he
does when he's about to leave me.

I'll ask around. Everyone shows up
on my side
of the sunset eventually.
I'll just Google him
and see.

And then of course he was gone. And leave it to Old Man to try
to blow my mind by suggesting you could find someone on the
other side just by Googling a name. But then that's Old Man
for ya.

Just then

the door opened

and I guess it was Fred
'cause he had a bucket and a mop. I was just sitting there
in a chair with my hands on my knees.
Fred looked surprised
but not too surprised. I guess he'd come to his janitor's closet before
and seen lots of unusual things.
It's okay, kid, he said. Finish up with whatever you're doing
and I'll come back in a few minutes.
And he left.
So I don't know if he thought I was doing drugs or whatever.
But it didn't matter
much, I guess.
Not to
Fred.

The End of the Day

No one said, Why did you miss class?
I went to English   then history
and then it was time to go home.
                    I looked around outside for Caitlan
but she was gone.   I wondered what she did after school.
I had
nowhere
to go but home.
                    So I went home.
When I went in the door   there was my mom
lying on the living room floor face up   eyes closed
                                        arms at her side.

Mom! I screamed.
          She didn't move   but she spoke:
                    What?
                              She didn't open her eyes.
Are you okay?   Yes.
She sounded annoyed.
What are you doing?

                              I'm meditating.
                              Just shut up so I can
                              meditate.

She was mad.
So I didn't say another word.
Went into the kitchen

for peanut butter
and celery.
Peanut butter is smooth on the tongue   and celery,
well, you gotta love celery: the way it crunches.

So after a few minutes
my mom
comes into the kitchen   and lights a cigarette.
       First one of the day, she says.
       I promised myself I wouldn't
       smoke
       until I meditated
       for twenty minutes.
My mom could take the longest drag
on a cigarette,
like half the cigarette
and then hold
the smoke
in her lungs.

       I chose not to say a word
       about secondhand smoke
       or any
       of that shit
       that would make her mad.
Instead, I said I was sorry
for messing up her meditation on the living room floor.
       It's hard, you know.
       Everything is hard

for a single mother
who's given up all
her addictions
except smokes
and alcohol.

I know, Mom, I said.
It can't be easy.

My Mother Knows

She knows that I love her
and would do just about anything for her
except buy her drugs.   She used to do that sometimes.
Give me money to buy her drugs   from this guy named
Chevy.   I liked Chevy.
Everybody did
even though he'd sell weed or coke or maybe even crack
to a kid like me
to take home to my mother.   Chevy bought groceries
                                for families
that didn't have any money,   usually because the father
                                or mother
                                had spent it all on drugs.

When we moved away—off reserve
Chevy gave my mom a whole
carton of smokes
as a going-away present.
This was after my father was gone.
I think my mom liked Chevy
but didn't want her kid
                having a drug dealer
                for a secondhand father.
I have to draw the line somewhere, she said.

And when we moved, she got real moody
'cause she gave up everything
but eventually went back to
nicotine and alcohol
in what she called "limited quantities."

She worried about me
and took me to counselors
and healers
and psychics.   I told them all about
Old Man   and they all told me
that was great.   The psychics said
they could see him.   But I don't know.

The psychics said I was an Old Soul and that part of me was
damaged because of some kind of shit that happened in a previous life. The not-talking routine that I did sometimes was a
good thing because the silence, they said, helped cleanse me
of negative energy from my past lives. I asked one of them,
Jack—Jack the side-burned psychic—if he could see Old Man
and he said he could, that Old Man was standing over my left
shoulder. And I turned and sure enough, Old Man was smiling.
But that was nothing new.

So Jack said Old Man would always be there for me. He also
said my father was somewhere Out West and kind of messed
up but would come back one day. He said he saw the two of
us as adults drinking beer in a gloomy bar. And there were no
other people in the bar. Just black dogs.

And I said,
Yeah,
that's probably
me
and him.
But the psychic said it was okay, that when I was an adult and
we had that beer together, we'd both be pretty messed up but
not totally fucked. And that, he assured me, was the way life
worked for most people, even Old Souls like me.

> You just got to work with
> what the spirit world hands you,
> and grow from there, he said.
> Isn't that true, Old Man? he asked.

And Old Man nodded, straightened his back and disappeared.
Then the psychic told my mother
> That will be a hundred bucks.

Cooking

My mother stopped cooking when
my dad left.
She said I had to cook from then on.
                                        I said I was okay with that.
So I shopped for food.
And cooked.
When my mom finished her cigarette
                                        she took out another
and just looked at it for a long while
                                        and then spoke to it:
You bastard, she said. Let go.
                        And then she put it back in the pack
and I asked her if she wanted me
to make
spaghetti.   I love you, kid, she said. Someday.
                                                        Someday.
But she didn't finish the someday sentence.
She never
does.
So I boiled water
and it got real steamy in the kitchen
and I kept thinking
I should expand our list
of stuff we would eat for meals.

Maybe start reading some of
those women's magazines
I saw in the supermarket line
with recipes
for artichoke salads
and sautéed eggplant
and thirty ways to lose weight
and fifty ways
to have great sex.

As I dropped in the spaghetti—
the really thin stuff
called capelli d'Angelo   angel hair
hair of the angels—
I told my mom about Caitlan.

Maybe I shouldn't have done that
                              'cause she pulled that second smoke
out from her pack
and lit it,
took the signature long drag,
tilted her head back
and said
Holy fuck.
Maybe
sending you to school
was a total
absolute
mistake.

The First Time He Walked Up to Me

I didn't know who he was at first.
        Just another guy at school.
              I didn't know what he wanted.
You're Jeremy, right?   I'd been walking down the hall
                  my eyes looking at the dusty floor
                  thinking about Geronimo
                  preventing the sun from coming up.
                  I looked up, nodded.
          Saw this skinny white kid
          pale, like a lot of white people when
          they don't get out in the sun
          with messy, kinda long hair hanging
          down over his eyes.
                  Yeah, Jeremy, I said.
We need to talk. You okay with that?
                  I thought maybe he was selling weed
                  and assumed I was a stoner.
                  What do we need to talk about?
              (The word "need" was freaking me a bit.)
Don't be scared.   Shit. I guess I looked scared.
                  I look that way a lot
         (even when I'm not scared).   So?
He looked puzzled now. Said, You can't tell that I'm different?
I wanted to say all white people kinda looked the same to me

but I received a knuckle sandwich for that one once.

Lesson learned.

Dunno, I said.

You don't know who I am?

Like what kind of bullshit, now?

How was I supposed to know who he was?

No, man. You somebody important,
someone famous?

No, dude.   (Nobody had called me dude in a long while.)

Who are you, dude?

Jenson Hayes, he said.

I guess I stopped breathing and stared.

You okay, dude? he asked.   I let out my breath and
took a new gulp of air.

I'm okay, I said. You?

He smiled a crooked smile, snorted a little.

Well, he said, you know, dude.

Yeah, We Needed to Talk

Can we go outside? he said.
I know you have a free period now.
So I followed him outside into some drizzling rain.
Dogs were barking somewhere.
There was a lot of litter on the sidewalk.
Why me? I asked.
Old Man said you'd help.
I laughed. Of course. What did he do, Google you?
Something like that, Jenson Hayes said.
He's very cool.
My grandfather invented cool.
Does Caitlan know
that you are around?

Not yet. But I saw you two
talking in Fred's closet.
You saw us? You were there?
Not exactly but ... you know.
I guess. Okay, so here you are.
Here I am and Old Man said
you'd be the one person
in the universe who would accept me
for who I am now
and not ask too many

bullshit questions.
I guess I could be that person.
But you really are ...
well ... you know?

> Yeah, he said, brushing the long hair
> out of his eyes.
> And in some ways it's all okay now,
> but in other ways
> it really sucks.

At least you don't have
to go to school, right, dude?

> > That's one of the perks.
> > But I miss a lot of things.
> > I miss being a vegan,
> > I miss trying to change the world,
> > and I even miss arguing with
> > greedy assholes.
> > I miss being who I was.

But at least you don't have to go to school
and you probably don't even have to
deal with assholes.

> > He nodded. True, but one more thing.
> > > I miss Caitlan.

What Love Is

Love, Jenson said, stays with you even if you move on. Love takes up a whole lot more of who you are than most people realize. You think you are all about arms and legs and your big fat brain with ideas and all those opinions—let me tell you, I was the king of opinions. And you think some things are important: like what to eat and what you look like and what people think of you and how you are going to make it through life and what kind of grade you are going to get on the final exam.

But none of that is important.

Guess you're right on that, I added.

So when me and Caitlan had this thing going,
I was stronger than I'd ever been before.
I mean strong and in a good way.
Nobody could get to me
like they had all my life.
Not my asshole father.
Not the mean teachers.
Not the creeps at school.
But then we had this
little argument,
Caitlan and me.
And we stopped
talking.
And I got stubborn.

Felt isolated.
All alone
and
weak.

He smelled it.
He knew I was weak.
He pretended to
be my friend.
Told me things about Caitlan that were not true.

                                        Who did?
Thomas Heaney.

                                        Paper Clip, I said.
                                        I call him Paper Clip.

He had some of his buddies
say all kinds of weird crap about me.
And Thomas
told Caitlan some stuff about me
that wasn't true.

I stopped going to school.
I should have been angry
and fought it.

                        Sometimes it's not that easy, I said.
Instead, I got weaker.
And then I got a text message
that came from
Caitlan.
At least it came from her phone

and it said
we were over
and she was going out with Thomas Heaney.

                    Fuckin' Paper Clip.

Just Standing Around in the Drizzle Talking to a Dead Dude

That pretty much sums up the situation
but I knew Jenson wasn't just here to shoot the shit.
So, Jenson, what now?
        I need you to help set things straight with Caitlan.
She can't hear you
or see you
like me?
        No. I tried. I really did.
She might not believe me.
She might think I'm damaged in the head.
Many people do. Lots of people.
        But she likes you, Jeremy.
She's pretty intense.
        That's one of the things I like about her.
Me too, I said,
although I realized now
that maybe he'd see
I really did "like"
her.
I guess you could
say I
had a

crush.

      I was thinking
      maybe I shouldn't
      get involved
with this Jenson Hayes.
      I guess Jenson saw the look on my face.

            Jeremy, he said. Old Man told me
            to tell you that you should
            always drink
            from the mountain stream
            and not
            city water.

Of course.
I knew what Old Man was saying.
Sometimes my grandfather
can be a pain in the ass.

            But we really have to do something
            about Thomas.

Revenge? I asked.
That didn't sound right.
My grandfather never
believed in revenge.
He never even spoke of getting revenge
against all the Europeans who stole our
land and fucked up
a sweet way of life.

            No, dude. Not revenge.
              We need to change him
              so he can see
                the light.

Back With the Living

Final period at school   French class
I am wondering why I am learning French
and not the language of
my grandparents.   Old Man
kept trying to explain to me when I was young
          that what language you use shapes the way you think.

English, he said, is
a language of things. Every *thing* has to have a name.
          Our old tongue
was better at showing relationships. Even people's identity
          showed connections.   Your name
in the old language would not be Jeremy Stone
                    but something else
and you would be
                    "Boy with strength and rock-hard courage
but kind heart."

I thought he was goofing
but maybe not.
OM also told me
there were no curse words
in our old language.

When you wanted to curse someone
and say something really unkind, he said,
you had to use English 'cause
                    there are so many really unkind words
                    in that language.
Language expresses the heart and soul of a culture,
he lectured to me when I was young
but he could tell I wasn't paying good attention.
                    Funny to think that that was
way back when
my grandfather still had a body
to put clothes on each morning.

                    Someday, he'd say,
I'll have to give back this ole body you see here.
It's only borrowed, he said,
to trap my spirit for a little while
so I can walk upright
and give advice to my
grandson.

Thomas Heaney in French Class

I knew it was too soon to confront
Paper Clip.   And I knew he'd be pissed
at me
for beating him fair and square in wrestling.

                          He saw me looking at him
and shot me
          a really nasty look. Silently mouthed something that
must have been Fuck You Indian.
Well, at least he didn't think I was Italian anymore.

                          Just then, Ms. Framboise
called on me
'cause I wasn't paying attention.
Monsieur Stone, she said, or perhaps you would be Monsieur
Pierre, Oui?
Monsieur Jerome Pierre sounds like the name of a Parisian
movie actor.

                 Paper Clip made a face and held his nose.
Ms. Framboise asked me a question in French.
I had
no clue
but I answered anyway

                          with something stuck in my
head from a previous class.
I said, La neige est froide aujourd'hui.

Which she told me later meant:

                              The snow is cold today.
Which was not the answer to the question.

                              The class laughed.
Paper Clip, I think, nearly peed himself.

                         I did my usual:
turned to stone, me Jerome Pierre,

                         and that's when I saw
Jenson Hayes sitting in what had been an empty desk over on
the side of the room near the windows.
He too was mouthing some words.

          And then the words were clear as a bell in my head,
so I added,

          Pardonnez moi, mademoiselle. Mon francaise est ter-
rible.   Excusez-moi.
And I could tell Ms. Framboise was impressed.
Jenson had given
me just the right thing to say
and everyone stopped laughing.
Hey, Jenson, I said silently in my head.

          Will you be there for me on the final exam?
          I could really use your help.

                    Jenson nodded but then I heard him say,
                    That's cheating, you know.
And I realized it was
but then having a dead dude give you answers for a final exam
seemed like
a cool way
to survive French.

The Troof

When I was young
                    the Th sound always came out like F.
I'm better now
but sometimes
I retreat and talk   like I did
                                             when I was
                                                    little.

But then, I still don't talk much;
mostly listen
and watch.

                                   I don't know why
but I don't think I was ever capable of lying.
                                   My mom
sometimes when she was high
in a weird way
(she wasn't always weird when high,
        sometimes she was funny, sometimes nice)
                                   but when it got ugly
she'd accuse me of stealing her smokes
or eating all the food in the fridge
                        Jeremy, come here, she'd screech
                        Did you do this?
No, Mom.

                        Are you lying to your mother?

No. I'm telling
the troof.
The troof.

> But she didn't always believe me.
> and she'd get weirder, angrier
> and more and more not-my-mom.

So I'd go ahead and say,
Yeah, Mom. I ate the food in the fridge

> (even though it was moldy sometimes
> and green and smelled bad)

and I stole your smokes and sold them to kids

> (which I would never do, believe me).

But my mom would hug me then

> and cry and say, I love you, Jeremy
> and I forgive you. I wish your father
> was here.

So I guess I was lying about
saying I never lied.
But my mom settled down mostly and got rid of all the really
bad addictions except smoking and drinking and sometimes
thinking too much about men. And my dad was still Out West.
And me
I was sticking with
the troof as best I could.

I, Jeremy Stone, swear to say the troof, the whole troof and
nothing but the troof, so help me God, which is why you have
to believe me when I tell you about Old Man and about Jenson

Hayes. I wouldn't, couldn't make something like that up.
Yeah,
so help me God.
And by the way,   God
please help me figure out
how I'm supposed to help Jenson.

The Troof Versus Paper Clip Heaney

I mean
I really didn't like the pressure,
didn't like it
when I knew
I HAD
to do something.
Me,
I prefer to hang back
and watch others
and let
things
happen.
I don't like
confrontation,
don't like
getting too involved,
don't like
getting
involved at all.
I
like
invisibility.

                              Sorry, dude,
                    Jenson said.

                    Sorry, but ... you know.
Yeah, I knew.

Personally, I think Old Man told Thomas
where I would be after school,
down walking along the little creek with
        the floating plastic pop bottles,
                old tires, and shopping carts
thinking that someday I'd come and clean this place up,
        get rid of the garbage
                and help this sad little creek out.
I guess I was just standing there listening to the water
talking to me
saying,
We know you, brother.
We flow down from the hills
where some of your dead relations
reside.
I felt less alone hearing that voice
but still kept feeling sorry for the stream
and staring at a couple of
used condoms
hanging from the branches of
birch trees.
                    And there was Paper Clip
                    with two other guys I didn't know.
                        That's Robert and Tyler,
                        Jenson said. A couple of
                                fucks.

I was thinking about Geronimo again
'cause his people had been ambushed
and then he fought back
with the same tactic.

                Jeremy Stone, right? Thomas said.
I nodded an Indian nod,
made my back straight.

                Worried?
About what?

                Us?
It was what you might call
kind of classic.
A scene played out
since
the beginning of
time.

                Right, Old Man suddenly said,
                like a bad TV show,
                like the old
                cowboys and Indians.
                Quick, change the channel.
So I told Thomas
(and Robert and Tyler)
the troof.

Jenson says
I'm supposed to
talk with you.

Who?

Jenson.
Jenson Hayes.

Paper Clip stared at me.
Robert and Tyler (those two very ordinary
looking white boys) looked puzzled.

You know.

Can't say I do. He some asshole
friend of yours?

Not really, I said.
Not when he was alive.

Whaddaya mean?

I sighed. I didn't ask
to get involved, I admitted.

Involved in what?

This?

What THIS is
is me coming here
to beat the crap
out of you.
(Thomas
was getting his old mean self
back in focus.)

Do you hate me?

Of course I do. We all do.
(Guess this meant Tyler and
Robert—
the Tybob twins.)

Do you hate a lot of people?

                    I hate people who are weak.

I'll take that as a yes.

                    I hate people who ...

I cut him off. Yeah, I said.
I know what you do to
people you think
are weak.

                    So?

So, I continue, Jenson says
you can't do that to anyone
ever again.

                    The two white boys were still puzzled.

                    Fuck Jenson.
                    You can't tell me what to do.

Of course not, I said.
You need to decide
that for yourself.
I'm only telling you
the troof.
And, yes,
it came out with
the F instead of
the Th   and I felt my breath
rushing out in a warm burst
between my
lower front teeth

and
my
top lip.

What Happened After That

I couldn't see him
but I heard Jenson's voice again.
Jenson told me that someone eventually found Caitlan's stolen
cell phone and a version of the text message sent to Jenson was
still on it. So I repeated that information to Tommy.
He's here now,
I added
just for flair.
Hey, I was now
writing the script
and I was tired
of cowboys and Indians.
Geronimo!

I still don't know why Thomas didn't beat the crap out of me
as in the original script. I don't think I fully got to him. But he
was confused the way people are when you rewrite the old cli-
ché story, especially when you bring dead people back into the
mix. Old Man kept coaching, saying, You're doing just fine, Jeremy. Don't be afraid.
And I wasn't afraid.
What could he do to me?
                              The phone thing was getting to him, maybe.

Evidence.
Paper Clip liked to sneak around
and do his nasty work knowing
he wouldn't get caught.

What cell phone? he asked.
I don't know about any
stolen cell phone.

But Jenson had nothing on this.
And Old Man just shrugged.
So I said squat.

And that
seemed to work.

Thomas Paper Clip
gave me the finger
and threatened me
with a look.
Tybob just stood there too
like they were waiting for
Thomas to tell them
what to do.

So I decided
to walk
ever   so   calmly
away.
My back was
to them
and they could have
tromped me

but they didn't.
And the sad little creek
just said,
You did good.
Just keep walking
and we'll watch your back.
So I silently told the creek I would come back someday soon
and haul those rusty shopping carts out of the water and clean
up all the garbage.

The flowing water just laughed.

What the Water Said Next

Good work, Jeremy.
Water runs downhill.
Maybe you can teach those boys
to take that hate they have
and turn the energy into something good.

        I was thinking that maybe it wasn't the
        water speaking but Old Man
        or maybe even Jenson Hayes

but the water (or whatever)
was reading my thoughts
and said,
Stoney,
it's all the same.
Spirit is spirit.

        Well, I didn't want to argue with that
                  but
I didn't think this thing was over with Thomas
and I wondered how he would ambush me next time.

        So what do I do now? I asked the water.

Go home
and make supper for
your mom.
She's not
feeling too good.

The Evening Meal

Yeah, my mom was pretty low. Depressed.
She was reading a book
called *A Woman's Guide to Mental Health*.
> Whoever wrote this book doesn't understand
> the first thing about women, she said.
> > Who wrote it?
> A man, she said.
> A doctor.
> He doesn't know
> diddly.

Well, I knew I had to do something to try to get my mom out of
her mood.

> > Lasagna, I said.
> > I'm going to make some
> > Lasagna.

She looked up at me
and smiled,
well,
tried to
smile.
How's school, Jeremy?

> > I got out the lasagna pan and

                              spaghetti sauce
                              and pasta.

I think I'm learning a little French, I said.
And psychology (although that wasn't really a school subject).

What does psychology say about depression?
                              I'm not sure
                              but maybe it happens when you feel
                              overwhelmed with everything.
Well, that's me.
Did you learn
how to fix it
so a person
can feel better?
                    I shrugged and continued to make lasagna.
                        They say drugs and alcohol don't work.
A little halfhearted laugh from Mom.
My son,
the genius, she said.
What else?
                    They say you have to stay busy, get involved
                    and cheer up.
                    Do you know if we have any mozzarella cheese?
You sound just like
your father.
Always changing the
subject to food
when he wants

to end a discussion.

                    Mom, can I try to call him tonight?
You want
to call your father?
How?

                    His cell phone.
He probably doesn't
have any minutes.
He probably doesn't
have any money
for minutes.

            I knew what she meant about the minutes.
            My dad could never pay regular monthly
                    bills for anything.
            But maybe he does have some minutes, I said.
And she smiled a real smile for once.
Yeah, who knows.
Maybe he has
some minutes.

Normal

Why can't we be like normal people? my mom asked over dinner. Why can't we be like those families you see on television?

> But she must have been thinking
> about the old days on television
> because nowadays there were
> no normal people on television.
> No normal families.
> Just fat families and homeless families
> and angry families that fought all the time.
> Families with money problems and
> families with really mean children.
> But there were a few funny families.
>> Mine was not one of them.

You make good lasagna, Jeremy. You take good care of your
mother. Do you know where my cigarettes got to?

> I went into the living room and found them
> and then handed Mom her smokes.

She took one out and stared at it again. I thought she would
start talking to it like she did sometimes and maybe that would
be our TV show: *Moms Talking to Tobacco*. "In this week's epi-
sode, Jeremy's mother gives a long-winded lecture to the dark
god of nicotine. Rated R."

>> Hah!

She didn't light it this time. The patch, she said. Maybe I'll try the patch. Thank you for making dinner. Now call your father. I don't want to talk to him. Not yet. But if he has enough minutes, tell him I want to talk to him soon. I gotta talk to him soon. Why can't we be a normal family?

Because, I said.

And I really didn't have to finish the sentence.

What the Raven Said

I had my dad's cell phone number in my wallet. It was written
on the back of a super lotto ticket he had bought for me.

He said, You'd have to split the winnings with
me if you win, Jer. We could go someplace
far away. Maybe take your mother with us if
she wanted.

This was after they'd already been living
in separate apartments.

But, of course, we didn't win. My father had said that a raven
had given him the winning numbers but when we didn't win
he said, Freakin' raven, anyway. Some of them are tricksters.
You can't trust those shiny black birds.

Which was a little funny because my father's name—
his real name—
was Smart Raven in our own language.

Not so smart, my mom would say. But he knows how to fly
away when he wants.
Yep.

Well, I dialled the number on the lotto ticket.

Hello.

Dad?

Jeremy?

Yeah.

Sheesh. Holy smokes.
It's good to hear your voice.

Where are you?

Out West.

Where Out West?

Right now, you mean?

Yeah.

I'm in a bar called the Golden Nugget.

Are you okay?

Yeah. A little sad, maybe. A little lonely.

Do you have minutes?

Yeah. I have minutes. Howzabout you?
Are you all right?

I think so.

Your mother?

Not so great.

Can I talk to her?

Not now. But soon.

She's not still hanging out
with that guy?
Whatshisname? Ford?

No. You mean Chevy. No, she isn't.

Good. Is she okay?

A little sad maybe. A little lonely. A little depressed.

Hey, he said, sounding
suddenly oddly cheerful.
Hey, me too.

I think you should come home.

              Come back East?

Yeah.

              But I got a job here.

A good one?

              Pay is real good.

Working on an oil rig, right?

              Sort of.

Whaddaya mean?

              I clean up after the guys on the oil rig.

              And back at the shop.

Do you like it? The work, I mean.

              I fuckin' hate it.

But the pay is good, right?

              Right. Hey, I got some new numbers

              from a raven out here. Maybe if I win …

If you win, you'll come home, I know.

              Yeah. Then a pause.

              Shit, I think I'm almost out of minutes.

And then he was gone.

Out of minutes.

Just like that.

The Phone That Never Rings

Our home phone that is.
Almost never rings except for telemarketers selling stuff we don't want or need.
But now it was ringing. My mother just looked at it. (She was still holding the unlit cigarette.)

> Don't bother answering it, she said.

But it might be Dad calling back.

> I don't know.
> No. Don't.
> She gives up, grabs a lighter,
> lights up.
> What the hell, she says,
> answer it if you want.

Dad?
Only it isn't Dad.

> Jeremy?

Yeah?

> It's me. Caitlan.

No way, I say to myself. Not in this lifetime. Caitlan calling me? My words have all flown away.

> Jeremy, are you there?

I'm here. (I cover the mouthpiece, mouth Caitlan's name silently to my mom and my mom rolls her eyes and leaves the room.)

How would you know this number?

        Ever hear of the internet?

You found my number on the internet?

        But it wasn't easy.

        You know how many

        Stones live in this town?

How many?

        Thirty-four. But you were

        only twenty-three.

        And that's my lucky number.

Wow.

        Like they say, leave no Stone unturned.

Huh?

        Sorry. It's just an expression.

Oh. I'm glad you called.

        Me too. I'm glad I found you.

        Can we meet somewhere?

Now?

        Yeah, now.

        Do you know where Coffee Coffee is?

Coffee Coffee is a coffee shop, right?

        Of course. It's two blocks

        from the school.

        Can you meet me?

Yes, of course.

        In a half hour. Okay?

Okay.

And she hung up. I don't know why the sound of a dead phone line was so beautiful. But it was a wonderful sound.

Coffee Coffee

I had to explain all this to my mom and she looked worried but said she understood and that she would not miss me at all but would sit down and watch a rerun of *Grey's Anatomy* on television even though all that blood in the hospital scenes gave her nightmares sometimes. But that I should go out and have fun on my date, only not be out too long and don't let that girl get me into any trouble.

What kind of trouble? I asked.

Trouble trouble, she said.

So I didn't say another word, but was wondering if Coffee Coffee was going to be trouble trouble. And I didn't know if that would be something that I liked or not. So I figured I would just have to wait and see.

It was a dark night
but warm
with a moon
coming up
like the one
I used to watch
back
in my community
in the woods.
As I walked, I
heard the sound of the phone line

after Caitlan had hung up.
It was an empty sound
and it created a space
where I could fill
in a lot of ideas I had.
Really nice ones.

Coffee Coffee was right where it was supposed to be.
Caitlan was inside
and looked prettier
than she did in school.
She sat alone
and when I walked up to her
she stood up and hugged me
and kissed me
on the cheek.
Everyone there watched
as my cheeks turned red.
                    I'll buy you something, she said.
                    What will it be?
I shrugged. I didn't really drink coffee but didn't want to sound
like a dweeb. Coffee, I said.
She laughed.   Two coffees it is.

Caffeine

Is a drug, she said. A good one. I love caffeine. You don't think
it's bad for you, do you?

> I sipped the hot black bitter liquid.
> No, I said, I don't think so.
> Look at all these people here
> drinking coffee. They look healthy.
> (Well, they really looked pale and
> unhealthy, like they had been living in
> caves for months and eating nothing
> but slugs.)

I guess you are wondering why I asked you to meet me here.

> I looked her in the eyes just then, a
> thing I don't usually do.
> You know, I said. Don't you?

Know what?

> About Jenson and me.

He contacted you, didn't he?

> I nodded, said, It was like he was right
> there. No different from you or anyone
> here.

Is that how it works for you?

> Sometimes. (But before it was only
> Old Man.)

Is he okay? Jenson?

I think he's all right but he can't let go.
That's what I was feeling. Jenson needs something. He needs our help. I think I still love him.

(I was afraid she would say that, but
there it is.)

So, I think that when you die with a lot of unresolved things—big things in your life—you hang around and try to find a way to finish things up.

He said he misses being a vegan,
he misses having arguments,
but he misses you the most.

I miss him too. And I don't know what to do about it. I can't quite give up on him either. Is he here now? Can you see him?

I looked around. No, I said. He's not here.
(Neither was Old Man which seemed
odd, because if I thought about Old Man, he'd
usually show up but maybe coffee shops were
not his thing. Or maybe caffeine
interfered with spirit.)

What else did he say?

I sipped my coffee and told her about the
thing with Thomas Heaney.

I've thought about ways to get back at him.

Jenson says no. Not the way to go.
Instead, we have to
show him the light.

The light?

You know. The light.

You show him the light, whatever that is. Not me. I'm still too dark to be anywhere near the light.

> At first I thought she was
> making fun of me and maybe
> ready to laugh at me,
> but there was more to it.
> Her dark was her pain.
> I could see it in her eyes now.

About Jenson, she said.
I'm thinking of
joining him.

> The words stung like wasps in my brain. No, I
> wanted to scream,
> to scream so loud. But I sat silent like a stone
> and waited.

You are the only one
I've told.
The only one
who
would
understand.

> I do understand, I said. (And meant it.)
> But Jenson would not want that.
> It's the last thing
> he would want.

How do you know? she asked.

> Because he's standing right behind you now.
> And he's saying this to me.
> To you.

She turned then, I think, really expecting to see a flesh and blood Jenson standing there in Coffee Coffee.

But he wasn't there.

> I had lied. I couldn't see him.
>
> Old Man, I pleaded inside my head.
>
> Old Man, what now?

But even OM was not there.

Just me

and Caitlan

and all that

dark.

Scars

I hadn't really noticed what Caitlan was wearing but
she suddenly unbuttoned her long sleeves
and showed me
her wrists.

> Scars.
> Three each
> on each arm.

> These weren't serious, she said.
> Kind of like
> practice.
> But it also helps with

> > the pain,
> > the dark.

Now I was really scared, but
tried not to show it. What
did you use? I asked.

> > I used
> > a razor blade.
> > I was very
> > careful not
> > to cut
> > too deep.

The most recent cut was not fully healed.

There was a scab
and a dark blue bruise under the skin
around the cut.

I wanted to run out of there, some place far from Coffee Coffee and never set foot in a coffee shop again. I wanted to get the hell away. I wanted to forget about Caitlan, about Jenson, about all the pale, pale people here and everywhere and go back to my old community. I wanted to stop talking again so no one would know my thoughts. I wanted the forest and the stream and the sun—the light inside the forest on a bright day—the sun shining through the maple and oak leaves and flashing through the white pine needles and the sparrows singing and the insects buzzing in my ears.

Caitlan buttoned her sleeves
and stared at me with
a truly frightened, crazy look.

I almost left her then. I was ready to just stand up and bolt out the door. And run.
But I heard a voice.

Hold your horses, Geronimo,
Old Man said.
You are a warrior, remember.
A warrior does not run when
he sees the enemy.

What enemy? I asked silently. Who is the enemy?

Old Man huffed.
Same old enemy you had
since you were little.

> You know—fear.
> Now quiet your mind
> and say something nice
> to Indian Eyes here.

I didn't know where to begin but Old Man was there making me sit up straight. (I felt his hand on my back.) And he was urging me to do something I never did, which was talk about my family and about me.

So I told her about my mom first and how she had been fighting her demons and doing an okay job of it by cutting her addictions down to just smokes and booze and the occasional fling with a man when she couldn't help herself. I told about finding her meditating on the floor and me thinking she was dead.

> That's when Caitlan interrupted
> and said, Yeah, I thought about that.
> I wouldn't want anyone I cared about
> to be the one to find me
> dead. Only strangers. That's why it's
> important to kill yourself someplace
> away from home, in a city somewhere.

Which seemed just about the saddest thing in the world to me and I said that. Man, I said, it's no good to be all alone in some strange city alive or dead. No good at all. (I was starting to get worked up here—maybe even angry that she'd consider doing this terrible thing.)

But I cleared my throat and sipped some more coffee which

now didn't seem so bad.

> Old Man was in front of me now,
> right behind Caitlan, shaking his head.
> Watch the caffeine, Jeremy. Too much
> caffeine gives you the shakes.

So I pushed the coffee cup away and focused on Caitlan again. Told her about my father Out West with not always having a lot of minutes on his phone. How phone conversations never ended with anyone saying goodbye, just the sound of being cut off and then static and eventually a dial tone or a woman's voice saying, please hang up the phone.

And I told her about the black dogs he spoke of. And how I had that image of me and him in the future in a grungy bar somewhere. And I think I was about to say something really important and meaningful but

> Caitlan cut me off. Jeremy,
> she said, her eyes dark and intense,
> Why are you telling me this?

I don't know, I said. I think it is because I care about you and want you to know who I am and to know that you are not alone. We all have messed up things in our lives and do our best to get on with it. (I know this sounds old and wise and that is definitely not me, Stoney Stone, but I was being coached by OM and he said it was okay to just let the words and stories spill out of me like water in a small mountain stream gushing over the rocks.)

And besides, I said (when the water started to slow down), besides, I really like you.

> Her look told me that liking
> someone was not a big deal.

I care about you.

> She still didn't say anything.

Maybe I—

> Wrong path, OM said.
> Don't go there unless you mean it.

love you.

What Caitlan Said to That

You're just saying that because you don't want me to kill myself. It's not real love. It's pity. And it's noble of you but it doesn't change the way I feel. Maybe I could have deeper feelings for you, too, but right now there is this big hole in my life with Jenson gone and I'm at least partly to blame for his death. And maybe I can join him this way. I don't really know how it works, but I know I just don't like it here anymore without him and I can't find a way to move on.

Stop, I said.

I'm your way

to move on.

I don't know. It's not that easy. Nothing is that easy. Everything is hard. Everything is not right. I can't just give up on Jenson. I can't just stop feeling what I feel. I can't just stop hurting. I can't just

What?

Keep living like this.

Old Man was shuffling around Coffee Coffee looking up at the fluorescent lights and cursing. Old Man always hated fluorescent lights.

When he was alive he had told me how much he had

hated fluorescent lights

(Even makes Indians look pale.)
and air conditioning.
(If the Great Spirit wanted us to
be cool all the time, he would
have given us free ice year
round.)

Let me help you, I said.

How?

You'll see, I said.
I smiled
and reached across the table and
took her hand in mine.
I leaned toward her
and accidentally knocked my
coffee over
but I didn't spill much.

Old Man straightened his back
and left.

The List

Alone at night in my room.
Now I had a list of things I had to do.
I don't like lists.
But there it is.

Help my mom hold it together each and every day.
Stay in contact with my dad and reel him home somehow.
Make Thomas Heaney stop being a cruel asshole.
Help Jenson move on.
Keep Caitlan alive.
Discover who I really am and why I am here.

All I could figure out was that the answer to the last item on
my list
was attached to all the items above it.

My head was spinning but I
made myself go to sleep
by imagining that I was not
a real person at all
but
the song
in the throat
of a sparrow.

Conference with Jenson

I took the long way to school
knowing I would be late
but focusing on my request
for Jenson to appear.
But he declined on the walk,
instead showing up
during lunch
when I was sitting alone
with a soggy
tuna fish sandwich
I had made
with way too much
mayonnaise.

> Jenson was there in front of me and said, I don't think
> you should eat tuna.
> Sometimes dolphins get killed by tuna fishermen. And
> they overfish.
> They use nets that get lost and swirl around the ocean
> capturing and trapping other fish that die. I just don't
> think …

I nodded towards the caf doors and led Jenson out into the
hall and then outside the school. There I promised to never
buy another can of tuna again, realizing one small joy had just
gone out of my life.

But I was glad to see Jenson.

I told him about Caitlan and he said he didn't know what she was going through.

> So I shouldn't be here, he said. I'm only hanging
> around for me. I somehow thought
> I could be with her and help her
> and also fix this other thing with Thomas.

I think, I said, you still have some kind of a hold on Caitlan. I think you need to somehow set her free and that, after a while, she will be okay.

> You say she's cutting herself. That's terrible.
>
> You think *I'm* doing this to her?

It's a funny business. I know it's her doing it to herself but I think she has to feel it inside her that you are moving on and don't want her to be with you. Does that make sense?

> Dude, not much makes sense but—

But maybe you have to try. Unfinished business needs to be finished even if—

> If what?

Even if it means letting go of someone you love.

Jenson was silent and I listened for the sound of the wind and maybe a bird or two but all I heard was traffic from the highway and announcements on the PA from inside the school.

> Maybe if I could just see her—
> if she could see me—one more time.
> Can you help me do that?

Why was he asking me this impossible thing to do?

No, I—

> I heard the bird sound first.

Then I saw him, Old Man
leaning against a No Parking
sign.
Jeremy, he said, I've been
meaning to tell you. You
are an Old Soul. Some would
call you a shaman. You can
do this maybe, with a little
help.
But it takes practice.

Hmm. Well.
Maybe I can.
But first I want
to try it
on Heaney.
If I can make him see you, you can convince him to change
                         (That would be one off my list, maybe.)
and then we try it
on Caitlan.

                    Jenson smiled.
                    Old Man smiled
                                but I saw
                                the worry
                                in his
                                dark eyes.

Another Sleeping Story

Usually I sleep like a log.
Head hits the pillow. Lights out.

Old Man always said that Indians had to move freely between the many worlds:

Wilderness, community, White Man's World (which he referred to as WMW), the world of the past,

the present, the future, dreamworld, and spiritworld.

Dreamworld and spiritworld are connected, but sometimes it's hard to sort out the dreams. If you are standing in front of math class in your underwear with everyone laughing at your shorts, you are probably not getting a real important message from the dream world.

But if you have a large eagle, say, speaking to you directly, then you should take it seriously.

Only it wasn't an eagle this time. And it was not Old Man who would sometimes show up in my dreams and play tricks on me or deliver advice.

This time it was just a skinny Indian kid named Jimmy. I knew who he was as soon as he appeared.

Jimmy was one of the little kids I used to wrestle with back in my house in the community. Jimmy always had a runny nose so whenever he wrestled you, you got snot all down your back. But I liked Jimmy. Everyone did. His full name was Jimmy Falcon, sometimes called JF by his dad.

Jimmy died of something when he was only eleven. And his mom, well, she went off the deep end and never really came back. His father spent three days in a sweat lodge until he said he made contact with Jimmy and he told everyone that Jimmy was in a good place and we should not be unhappy. Then Jimmy's father sat down and started eating the moose meat and bannock and potato salad that had been prepared for him by the neighbors. He ate more potato salad than seemed humanly possible.

But Jimmy had not appeared to me until that night, lights out, full asleep.

> Stoney, he said. (He had always called me that.) Stoney, they asked me to deliver some news to you.

I wanted to say, Hi Jimmy, good to see you, but couldn't. I can hardly ever speak in those dreams. Maybe you aren't allowed to have vocal cords in dreams.

> Relax, he said, and let me do the talking.

I relaxed just like he said and he came much more clearly into focus. Hadn't changed a bit.

> We know about your list.

I'm still not sure who "we" were but I was pretty sure this was a spirit dream and not just an underwear one.

> The reason this is all coming down the pike at you
> is because you are an Old Soul

(I knew that part)

> and because you are a healer. A fixer.
> A guy who needs to set things right.

(Shit, I was thinking. That's way too much responsibility. I can't hardly keep myself together. How can I heal others?)

> I know, I know. It sounds like a bit much.
> And I haven't been on your side of the line
> in a while
> so I can only guess what it's like these days.
> I can see, though, that you have more baggage than
> me. Dying young has its advantages.

Jimmy was always the one to see the upside of everything. You go fishing and catch no fish and Jimmy would say, At least we got to sit by the river and avoid doing homework. Or if his dad's car broke down, Jimmy got to hang out with his father and have a father and son car fixing talk. Etc.

> And I think you are right about Paper Clip.
> If you can get him on the right path,
> that would be a good start.
> One less asshole out there hurting people.
> You'd be surprised at how one
> Thomas Heaney can do so much damage.
> Like a snowball rolling downhill.

I'm wondering how. How do you convert a Paper Clip? And why is that so important?

> I know. You're wondering how. And why.

I guess this is when I was reminded that the Jimmys and Old Man can probably hear my thoughts. And oh shit to that.

> Oh shit is right. But don't give it a second thought.
> Look, I don't have a body to worry about.
> You are still in the physical realm, so to speak.

Okay, okay. But I still wasn't sure where to begin.

> You begin by tuning in to Paper Clip

and then do something kind for him.

Something he can recognize as

a kind thing in his world.

Like what?

Like cheating. PC is terrible at tests.

He has test anxiety.

Paper Clip?

C'mon, it stands to reason.

He is like he is because he's so freakin' insecure.

He's scared of his own shadow.

It's why he hangs out with Tybob. It's why he picked on Jenson.

You got a test tomorrow in European History, right?

I'd forgotten to study for it with all the other stuff going on.

Don't worry. Jimmy will be there.

I got all the answers.

I'll be there to share them with you.

So you share them with Thomas Heaney.

Wherever he sits, sit beside him.

And let him cheat off me?

It's not really cheating. I mean, if you can see the big picture. You'll get the hang of it after a while. There's a lot of shades of gray about what's right and what's wrong. Trust me. You'll be a great healer and a fine shaman.

The French Revolution

Yes
there was that   test
in European History   that Jimmy seemed to
                                                  know all about.

Funny thing, I guess: me a North American
Aboriginal studying things like
the French Revolution.   So many wars in Europe
                                         to memorize and figure out.

And really, what was the point?   But it was school.
So go figure.

                              I had read the book
                              but it didn't stick.
The words had a habit of running away,
                         none stayed in my head
                              so I hoped Jimmy wasn't
                              bullshitting.
(And it was going to be hard to concentrate,
worrying about Caitlan.
But she promised me she wouldn't
off herself until we talked about it more.
But I still couldn't stay focused on the French Revolution.)
I had the set up: let Thomas Heaney
                              sit down first and then
                              take the desk next to him.

You'd have to see

that look he gave me:

I think you could safely call it "Pure Hate" if it was a painting
on the wall with a title.

I smiled.   (What else can an Indian do?)

Fuck off. Just fuck off,

he said.

Mr. McLeod said, Okay, students, today the test is going to be a
simple one with two questions:

What were the causes of the French Revolution?

What were the results of the French Revolution?

He turned his back and wrote them on the board.

You can answer

in point form.

Now begin.

Everyone moaned like we were being tortured.

Paper Clip gave McLeod the finger

but McLeod had his back turned and didn't see it.

Heaney didn't have any paper so I gave him three sheets of
lined paper.

(Whenever I think of school, I think of those pale blue lines on
binder paper. And I always had a hard time keeping my letters
inside those lines. But that's just me.)

Reasons for the French Revolution?   *Bad leaders, unhappy*
                                          French people.

Results of the French Revolution?   *More bad leaders, more*
                                          unhappy French people.

I figured McLeod wanted more, but that's all I had even though
I had read the textbook.

Yo, Jimmy.

Sounds of pens and pencils scratching on paper. Sounds of people knowing answers.

> Not Thomas who was picking his nose
> like it was the most important thing
> in the world.

Yo, Jimmy. I need ya, buddy.

> Hold your horses, Jimmy said
> inside my brain.
> I'm here already.

He was still just eleven.

I hope you know your shit about this French thing, I said silently.

> Well, I got access to the information.

Like Google, right?

> Pretty much but better. I got whatever
> you need.

So it pretty much came into my head like I was copying it off the internet.

(I know, I know. It's still cheating. But cheating for a good cause. You have to stay focused on the big picture. This was all about getting PC to like me.)

> Here goes, Jimmy said.

So I just let my pen slide over the page and tried to stay within the parallel lines

double spaced as Mr. McLeod would have it.

There were a number of causes of the French Revolution that began in 1789:

1. *there were many poor unhappy people*

2. *Louis XVI and his ministers were unpopular*

3. *new ideas about freedom and democracy were being spread*

4. *the French were inspired by the American Revolution.*

5. *there was too much taxation of the 5 million French peasants*

   > *10% to the church*

   > *5% property tax*

   > *and taxes on wine and baked goods*

6. *nobles and church leaders didn't have to pay tax*

7. *there were crop failures, poor harvests, and it was illegal to grow potatoes*

8. *people were starving*

Jimmy, are you sure it was illegal to grow potatoes?

> Yep.

Why, dude?

> The rich people called it "dirty food."

'Cause it came out of the dirt?

> The rich people back then
> were pretty well fucked up.

I saw that my writing was very neat and orderly and even readable, which must have been Jimmy's doing and not mine.

> Thomas had a nice clean white sheet
> in front of him
> and seemed to be studying a pimple on
> his cheek with his index finger.

Mr. McLeod was reading a book and really not watching us. So now was the time.

I slipped my answers over to Thomas.

He didn't know what the fuck was going on.

I smiled and nodded to my answers.

> He thought it was a trick.

I smiled some more, gave him a thumbs-up.

> He looked at McLeod and
> then he started writing.
> Well, copying.

On a second sheet of paper, I got on with answer two about the results of the French Revolution.

I won't bore you, but Jimmy gave me stuff about the end of feudalism, executions, violence, democracy, and more rights for the peasants, but then there were wars and Napoleon and more wars.

I handed that one to Thomas too.

At the end of class we both handed in our work.

> Thomas didn't say anything to me.
> Just looked stunned.

I smiled and gave him two thumbs up.

> Jimmy just said, Watch what happens next.

What Happened Next

Was   we

got caught.

Two hours later,

Mr. McLeod had us called to the vice principal's office.

Our teacher sat there with his arms folded.

Ms. Goldworthy, the VP,

looked like she had eaten some bad yogurt.

McLeod kind of went into a rant. He was enraged at both of us.

Paper Clip looked meanly at me.

He thought I did this on purpose to nail

his ass to the wall.

Ms. G wanted to "get to the bottom of this."

McLeod did too.

Jimmy was nowhere around.

The big question is, Ms. G said,

who copied from whom?

(You don't usually hear anyone actually use the word "whom"
much anymore, I was thinking.)

Paper Clip sat sullen.

He was used to getting blamed for
things.

You could tell he had a strategy for
times like this:

don't own up to anything

and blame someone else
and say you are the victim.

Me, I confessed,

said it was me who cheated.

(Well, I did. I didn't know the answers. Jimmy had given them to me.)

Is that true? McLeod asked.

Yes. Absolutely.
I'm sorry.

Thomas looked baffled.

Ms. G nodded a kind of approval. Have you
cheated before? she asked.

No. never. (The truth.)

Why now? she wanted to know.

Well, I began, it was this whole European history thing. I kept wondering why we weren't studying
something more important.

(And I wasn't sure where I was going.)

Mr. McLeod suddenly looked up.

Oh, he said sympathetically, you mean like ...

I sat silently.

Um, he continued, like the history of
your people.

I nodded.

Then there was just this big load of silence
sitting on us all.

Thomas now nodded as well. He too acted like
we'd been cheated out of learning about the
true history of Aboriginal North Americans.

He'd become a Native rights advocate
in twelve seconds.
Well, Ms. Goldworthy finally said,
I think that if Jeremy promises
not to
ever cheat again
we should
put this behind us
and
we should all

move on.

Which we did.
I still got the F.
But I had turned the corner
with Paper Clip.
Pretty soon,
it would be time
to introduce him
to Jenson.

Caitlan in the Hall

She had heard I'd been called to the office,
                        grabbed me as I walked out.
            Thomas turned and looked at her,
                                    at me.
            He looked baffled, befuddled, bewildered.
        Jeremy, what's going on? Why were you in there with
        Thomas?
        What did he do now? Are you okay? Are you in trouble?
        Did you try to kick his ass? I need to know.
I had lost my speech again, just then. She was tugging at my
arm. All I knew was that Caitlan cared.
She was worried about me.
This girl cared.   When I could muster enough
oxygen in my lungs
I tried to explain.
            That doesn't make sense, she said. You let him copy?
            You took the blame? You covered for him?
Yes, yes, and yes.   It was Jimmy's idea.
            Jimmy. Who's Jimmy?
Well ... sure, I opened up and told her about Jimmy.
It's all part of the plan, I said.

Truth is, I wasn't the type of person who made plans. Things
happened or didn't happen. I just usually went along for the

ride.

Jimmy begins with a J, Caitlan said to me.

So?

Jimmy, Jeremy, Jenson. Three names beginning with J.

So?

It just seems curious, she said. Very curious.
Can you introduce me to Jimmy?

No, no, and no,
Jimmy insisted.

I guess not, I told Caitlan.

Why not?

I don't know. Jimmy says no.
He's only eleven
and shy around girls.

I noticed that Caitlan was wearing a long-sleeved blouse buttoned at the wrists.

How are you doing? I asked.

I'm hanging in there. But it's very dark inside.
Inside me, I mean.
What about Jenson?

Soon, I said.
I promise.
Soon.   (Then we stopped walking.)

Did you hear about the earthquake in South
America? she asked suddenly.

No.

I saw the pictures on TV. It was awful.

Probably not a good idea to watch that stuff. There's a lot of trouble in the world. Hard enough to ...

(She cut me off.) I can't help but watch.

I take in other people's pain.

It's what I do.

I had a couple of my own psychology textbooks of advice for her about that. Not the professional type of books, just the Jeremy Stone authored versions with advice like: don't go there, don't take on others' suffering unless you can do something about it, don't watch the news ever, don't increase your own darkness with the world's catastrophes, etc., etc.

I gotta go to physics, she said.

We're doing Einstein today. I love Einstein.

(At least that was positive.)

I wondered why she was taking physics. It didn't seem like a Caitlan thing to do.

I love Einstein, too, I said. I really like his hair and his ideas.

She was walking away and I tried to keep up. For this brief instant, her darkness was gone.

Like someone
had switched on
a light in a very
dark room.

But
there
was
something
not quite
right about

mixing earthquakes
and Einstein.

Waiting for Paper Clip

I thought it would be better
if he came to me
rather than me trying to approach him.
It didn't take long.
He found me by the creek. I had just hauled out
an old truck tire
and was splattered with black, stinky muck.
He was alone. (No Tyler, no Robert)
You are one crazy, totally insane
piece of work, PC said.
I was rubbing black oily mud from my hands onto my pants.
(Something about the feel of wet sticky mud on my hands
though felt good, not bad. Something from a previous life may-
be.)
I did what I had to do, I said.
Who made you do it?
So, for the second time
I explained about Jimmy.
He talks to you?
(Thomas seemed genuinely curious.
There was no hostility in him now—
a completely changed Clip.)
He was an old chum. From when I was little. And then he got
sick and died.

And now he comes back to haunt you?

Not haunt.

What then?

Advise.

Oh. (Thomas didn't know
what to say next, I guess.)

I took the leap.

So does Jenson.

Who?

Jenson Hayes, you know?

A puzzled look again. Not a clue.

I was thinking of Jimmy's plan.

This was the next step right?

What should I do?

I put my muddied hand to my cheek and rubbed the
mud in.

But maybe it was too soon.

But it *had* to be soon. Caitlan would lose interest in
Einstein

and go back to watching earthquake victims and
thinking about Jenson.

I know what happened, I said.

I know why Jenson killed himself.

Who the fuck is Jenson?

(Some loss of cool on PC's part.)

Jenson Hayes, I repeated.

A kid in your class,

hung out with Caitlan.

I stay far away from that crazy bitch.

(He was rattled again.)

And I never knew anyone named Jenson.

Okay, I told myself. I pushed things this far. He doesn't want to own up. I could understand he was covering up what happened. Didn't want to get involved.

Thomas Heaney took a deep breath.

Jeremy, he said, go home and get cleaned up.

You look like you've seen a ghost.

Mud and Mom

My mom took one look at me. You got into a fight, didn't you?
> No, I was at the creek.

Look at your face, your pants. Jeremy, sometimes I think you'll
never grow up.

> My mom found a towel, wet it, and started to clean
> my face.

> I didn't smell any cigarettes or booze on her breath.

When you were born, she told me, you arrived way too early.

> I knew this story but did not want to stop her.

The doctors didn't think you'd live
and they kept telling me to prepare myself
in case you didn't.
But I wanted you to live so badly.
You were so tiny and in an incubator
and your father and I would stand there leaning over
and listen to your breathing—a faint gurgling sound—
and sometimes you would stop—I don't know what it was—
it was like you'd stop, you were giving up,
and I'd say, Please God, let him take
another breath.
And you did.

And then you were home with us,
not healthy, but home

and I promised God
I would
clean up
my act.

But I
didn't exactly
do that.
And
God
was
kind
anyway.

Now, go take a bath.

God in the Bathtub

I hadn't thought much about God for a while. But in the bath-tub, with the hot water running in, I thanked God for allowing me to live as a baby. And I wondered where I would be now if I had not lived through those early premature days of being alive. Maybe I'd be a tree in a forest or a rock in a clean running stream. Or another person in another time and place. An Old Soul on his next adventure.

Maybe I had been close to death or actually died and come back all those times I stopped breathing. I held my breath now and slipped down into the warm bath water. I held my eyes tightly shut and waited for all the oxygen to burn up in my lungs and waited for answers to come.
But they didn't.
Only pictures:
the sun,
the light filtering green through spring leaves,
and then black space with a bunch of patterns of many colors.
I couldn't recognize the patterns exactly
but I think I saw symbols
like the ones my people
used to carve into rocks.
And then I saw
the sun again.

And surfaced and took
a deep breath.

And it was quiet in my head: I was alone.
No Jenson.
No Jimmy.
No Old Man.
Alone with my thoughts,
which told me
something
was not
quite
right.

My Mom in the Kitchen Staring at an Unopened Pack of Smokes

Yes, she'd do this sometimes.

A test.

One she almost always failed.

The patch, she said. I'm going to try the patch again. Look at you, all clean. No more mud. Did you know in the old days, some of the people would coat themselves with mud while fishing to keep the mosquitoes and black flies from biting them.

Did it work?

It must have. I never tried it. I used Muskol instead. Or sometimes I could use my mind to keep the bugs away. When I was young and innocent. That is what my grandmother said to do. She claimed she could use her mind and that never once in her entire life was she bitten by a mosquito.

Do you think it was true?

No. I think it was just a story. My grandmother told me lots of stories when I was little that I soon learned were bullshit. But it was really good bullshit and made me love her more for it. It's what we believe that shapes who we are and what we believe is not necessarily true.

I'd been thinking a lot about Jimmy
and why he had appeared now in my life so

this seemed like as good a time
as any to mention this to her.
I think you can buy cigarettes made from lettuce. Maybe I
could smoke them while on the patch.

Mom?
Yes, Jeremy.
You remember Jimmy?
Jimmy Talltree who ran the little store back in the community?
No, Jimmy Falcon.
I don't remember Jimmy Falcon.
(This seemed impossible
but then maybe my mom had lost some
memory. There had been a lot of drugs.)

Jimmy and I were friends. He used to
hang out at
our house all the time. Skinny little
kid. Always had a runny nose.
Could have been any one of your friends, I guess. But I don't
remember him.

Remember, he died when we were
both eleven?
Eleven?
He got sick and didn't get better.
Holy fuck, my mom said.
What?
Jimmy?
Yeah.
Jimmy was the name you gave to your imaginary friend. The
one you had since you were really little.

No, Mom. He was a real kid like me.

She reached for the pack of cigarettes, broke open the cellophane, and took one out.

She shook her head. We thought you'd never give up on him, she said.

That can't be right.

She lit up the cigarette. Sorry, she said. It's one of those times.

Think hard. Jimmy Falcon.

We used to wrestle in the living room.

When you were eleven, my mom said, staring at the smoke she exhaled,

your grandfather died

and your father went off

the deep end.

And you kept asking me

What happened to Jimmy?

And I just had to keep repeating,

I don't know, Jeremy,

I just don't know.

Awkward Moments in the Kitchen

Let's face it, my mom screws up a lot of things and makes lots of mistakes. She'd be the first to admit it and I always forgive her. Like I say, she did a whack of drugs. I couldn't name them all but she had memory lapse and sometimes got confused and called me by different names. So this could have been one of those times. Unfortunately, she said this:

> Jeremy, I'm clear as a bell on this.
> You made Jimmy up
> and I went along with it 'cause
> it helped to keep you happy.
> Otherwise, you'd get so lonely
> and sad
> after your grampa passed.

I couldn't remember my grandfather dying.
I guess
when he died
he came right
back.
Old Man
never
left.

> Maybe we need to take you
> back for more tests.

I don't
want
any
more
tests.

          Your doctor said you
          were cured
          when you told him to fuck off.

I had only
stayed
silent
because
I
didn't have
anything to say.

          I understand that perfectly.
       Whatever can be said has probably
            already been said by someone.

Mom?

          Yeah, hon?

You telling me the truth about Jimmy?

          Big exhale of smoke. A whole
          cloud of it.
          My mom opens a window.
          Nods yes.
          But I was glad you had Jimmy,
          she says.
          Every kid needs a best friend.

Back to the List, the Plan

Me in my bedroom wondering why Old Man is not nearby to
help me with this one.
Old Man?
Nothing.
So (gulp) Jimmy Falcon was from my imagination.
From my subconscious.
Told me to help Thomas cheat,
gave me the answers,
and disappeared.
(Just as a test, I called out inside my mind.)
Jimmy! Help me!
No Jimmy.
Maybe once you have doubt about something, someone from
the other place,
they go away
and you're left
alone
with no one
to talk to
but people
who are living.
(I didn't want that.)
Damn.
(My brain is latching onto something now. I feel a kind of

panic. I'm forgetting how to breathe.)

Oh fuck.

Paper Clip.

What did he say?

Suicide for Amateurs

No, not me.
I'm thinking about Jenson Hayes.
I'm hoping my computer doesn't work so I don't have to do
this.
But it's on, the wireless is working.
I Google Jenson Hayes
and get a shitload of hits.
Thank God.
But
the first Jenson Hayes is a champion long-distance cyclist,
another a lawyer from Baton Rouge, Louisiana,
one is a Grand Prix race driver,
another is an architect in Pocatello, Idaho.
(I feel the panic rising like a lump in my throat.
Be cool, Stoney. There's always someone, many people,
with the same name. It's a small planet with a lot of
people and not enough names to go around.)
I type in *Jenson Hayes Suicide*
and get a whack of stuff
but nothing about Caitlan's Jenson.
I type in his name again
and the name of our town
(and hesitate—there has to be something; it must have been in
the papers, in the news).

My finger hovers.
(Old Man, where are you? I know you hate computers but
could you hang with me on this one?)
Fuck.
Click.

More stuff:
Jensons and suicide,
Hayes and suicide,
but nothing I can find
(as I scroll down
twenty pages of
web listings)
about the Jenson Hayes
I know.

The World According to Jeremy Stone

I want to call Caitlan and ask some questions.

I want all this to make sense.

I want to ask Thomas Heaney some more questions about Jenson. (Of course, he was lying.)

I want to find some of my old childhood friends. (Yes, I'm sure I had real friends. I wasn't always lonely.)

I want more answers from my mom about Jimmy. Maybe she can't remember 'cause of the drugs.

I want something.

Something. (I smash my fist into the keyboard.)

                                                        And then

                                Hold your horses,

                                Old Man says. Just

                                hold your horses.

Where were you? I demand. Why couldn't I find you?

                                There's no easy answer to that.

Don't give me that bullshit. (I've never ever said anything like this to my grandfather before.)

                        Well, if you must know, I was away. Kind of a retreat.

                        I'd been advised I was too attached to my past,

                        to the people I love. That includes you.

But I need you.

                                I know, Stoney.

                                So don't worry. I'm not

going anywhere.

I could see there was something different about him but couldn't quite place it.

Maybe it wasn't him. Maybe it was me. Something different about me.

I was full

of doubt.

Jenson, I said. What about Jenson? I'm not sure there ever was a Jenson.

Well, that's true and not true.

You're using doublespeak.

I know what you mean.

It's just that sometimes you have to hold two

opposing ideas in your head

at the same time.

Bullshit.

I know. Maybe it's like your mother's

cigarette smoke. You can see it, you can smell it

but you can't reach out and grab it.

Maybe it's like that.

I sat silently. I'd always, always trusted anything Old Man had ever told me.

But it was you who introduced me to Jenson.

And I spoke with him.

Did you just put him in my mind? Did you make him up?

No.

Did I create him like some kind of hallucination?

No, Jeremy.

Caitlan invented

Jenson Hayes.

But you helped me buy into her ... what?

Illusion?

I did what I had to do.

You did this to help her?

In some ways, yes.

And to help you, too.

But Jenson seemed as real as anyone.

As real as Thomas Heaney.

As real as Caitlan.

As real as Jimmy?

Yes.

Jimmy was all yours. Not mine.

But they both seemed as real as ...

As me?

Yes.

Old Man looked very old now, older than I'd ever seen him.

You're gonna have a hard time sleeping tonight.

So I'll stay in that chair there while you sleep.

And this will all make sense in the morning?

Old Man tried to straighten his back but went right back to being hunched over.

Like someone had put a heavy load on his shoulders.

No, he answered. Probably not.

Crazy Horse

I don't know if I was actually asleep
or whether Old Man did something
but I was not in my room. I was
on top of a hill surrounded by brown
dry hills beneath a bright sun.
And Old Man was walking towards me.
He looked a lot younger.
This is better, he said. We'll start here.
Let me tell you about Crazy Horse.

He was born near here and was a warrior and great leader.

Like Geronimo?

Yes.
See that bird.

A red-tailed hawk flew toward us and then away.
Let's go, Old Man said. Crazy Horse followed a red-tailed hawk
one day and he had many visions.

We started walking south.

Following the bird, Crazy Horse went into the spirit world
where he could see that the spirit world was the real world and
the physical world was just like a place made up of shadows of
the spirit world.

In that spirit world, Crazy Horse was told that he could move
freely between the two worlds if he needed to do so and that

when he was going into battle, he could slip out of the physical world and see what was going on behind it all to understand what was really going on. That way he would not get injured and he would be safe.

He was told that he needed to be the protector of his people and that he'd have help from the spirits of his ancestors. He was to keep an eye out for a white owl that would be around to help protect him.

Later, he was also given a black stone from a man named Horn Chips, a medicine man, and he put that stone behind his horse's ear to protect the horse and make man and animal become one in battle.

> But he was killed, right?

Not before he had been in many battles and become a great warrior. We all have to give our bodies back to the earth eventually. He did what he needed to do and then he moved on.

> It was about then that I thought I was going to wake up.
>
> But I opened my eyes and realized
> I had not been asleep.
> It had been some kind of trance, maybe.
> Old Man, the older Old Man, was sitting there
> beside my bed in the dim light of morning.

I'm not saying you should be engaging in battles like Crazy Horse or Geronimo. That time is past.

Today, it's kinda complicated being a warrior. It's not about fighting your enemies anymore.

It's about conquering your fears, conquering yourself, and protecting what needs to be protected.

> Protect who from what?

He laughed. It varies, he said.

Sometimes it means learning to help someone protect themselves from what is within.

The Bird

The bird outside my window
was not a red-tailed hawk
or a white owl.
It was a small
brown
sparrow
with a
very
ambitious
song.

Saturday: Caitlan Day

Think of it as a quest, I told her.
>> She looked sullen, a little crazy, pale
>> but she still had those
>>> beautiful Indian eyes.
There is a petroglyph not far from here, I said.
>>> A what?
A drawing in stone. Put there by ancient peoples.
>> Jeremy, you've been playing
>> too many video games.
I don't play video games.

>>> Then what is this?
A quest.
We are searching for something.
>> I don't know. I don't feel good.
I know. But trust me.
>> I held her hand.
>> She looked scared.
>> I felt the scars on her hands,
>> an unhealed cut deep in the palm of one hand.
>> Jeremy, what about Jenson?
We'll talk about Jenson.

>> We took a bus

that went almost all the way
to my old community.
When we got off
Old Man was there
sitting on a bench
reading a newspaper.
I hadn't expected that.
He smiled at us.

You know him? Caitlan asked.

Yep. That's my grandfather.

Caitlan understood.

I wasn't sure how we would find the trail to the petroglyph,
I said. (This was true. I was waiting for guidance. But here it
was.)

He'll show us the way.

Old Man smiled some more.

I could tell he wasn't going to speak, though.

I saw the doubt
in Caitlan's eyes.

It's okay, I said. I think he's here to help us find Jenson. (Don't
know for sure why I said that, but I did.)

We hiked through some dense bush on a trail that didn't seem
much like a trail. It had been overgrown with alders and maple saplings. And then we came to a bare ridge of rock that led
higher up the hill until there were no trees at all. Just a bare
ridge of bedrock running north and south.

I was breathing hard.

Caitlan was breathing hard.

Old Man had kept walking faster and faster, getting farther and
farther ahead of us.

And then he was far away and we couldn't see him.

Maybe he was gone.

I heard a sparrow singing.

And then I looked down.

It was faint, hard to make out at first, worn down by a thousand
years of weather, covered with lichen.

But I'd been there before as a boy

with my grandfather

when he was alive.

I brushed away some lichen and moss.

I see it, she said.

A star.

North, south, east, and west.

What does it mean?

I'm not sure, I said.

But it was put here a long time ago

because this is a sacred place

of spirits.

Caitlan traced the lines

in the rocks with her finger.

And that's when we heard someone

walking our way.

What the Sparrow Saw

The sparrow was still singing.
I saw him now on the prickly limb
of a low, scrubby pine tree.
He flew off to the south
when Jenson walked by.

                                  Caitlan swallowed hard.

                                           Jenson?

       I don't know if I should be here, he said
       But I followed you.
I was wide-eyed but said nothing.
I pretended I was not afraid.
I thought of Geronimo coaxing the sun to come up later,
Crazy Horse understanding the real world behind the shadow
world of the living.
I silently said, Holy Fuck, Old Man, you are really messing with
us now.

           Old Man only said, "Shush" inside my head.

Jenson Speaks

I wanted to sort this all out in my head and make sense of what
was going on but realized it was way beyond my control or my
full understanding or any of that shit.
Sit back and let things roll.

Caitlan walked right up to Jenson
and I expected him to vanish like Old Man had.
I thought it was all some kind of trick,
some kind of weird dream
but it wasn't like that.

Caitlan turned to me. Jeremy, she said,
would you mind leaving us here
alone for a bit?

I looked at Jenson, tried to fathom who he was, what he was,
what his intentions were, tried to figure out if Caitlan was in
danger, if we were both complete psychos, if it had really been
Old Man leading us, and worst of all, wondering how could
Jenson be here if he never existed in the first place?

Shush, Old Man told me.

I nodded, walked north in the direction Old Man had gone,
followed the ridge of granite into the bush on what I knew was
once a well-travelled path of my ancestors, expecting any min-
ute to see a hawk or an owl, but there was nothing.
Only black flies and a few mosquitoes that attacked me
because they knew a truly confused boy

was no warrior but just easy prey
and a good source
of blood.

I sat down on an outcropping of rock
and looked down at the valley below—
my old community.
I saw the house I had been born in,
thought of my childhood,
my family,
and how
so much had changed,
how much I had lost,
thought maybe I was
in some kind of stupor again
like the night before,
wondered why Old Man
wasn't there
to comfort me,
to tell me it was all
going to be okay.
I waited for a sign,
some signal,
some voice inside my head,
some image in the sky
but I got nothing.
I felt small
and insignificant
and left behind.

I lost my courage and slipped into a dark place
where I was all
alone.

And then I heard hurried footsteps
and shallow, fast breathing.

                                                    Jeremy.
I stood up and Caitlan fell into me, wrapped her arms around
me.

                    She was crying.

                              Jenson explained everything,
                              she said.
                              I'm sorry. I didn't mean
                              to put you through all this.
                              To drag you in.
You okay?

                              Not yet, she said.
                              But I will be
                              soon.
I wanted to ask about what happened
back there at the petroglyph.
I wanted to know the whole story.
But my grandfather's gentle, invisible hand
was over my mouth
and he was shushing me again
and assuring me
that words
didn't always
work.

Language

I stopped speaking again after that.
Like Old Man had said,
words don't always work.
> So, Mr. Silence, what is it this time?
> my mom asked.
Everything, I wanted to say,
Everything and nothing.
> Guess everyone has a right
> to clam up sometimes.
> Maybe we should go see that shrink again?
I shook my head, no.
> How about Jack the sideburned psychic?
Sure, I nodded, why not.

When we got to the office an hour later
JTSBP took one look at me and said, Oh boy, this kid has been
through the wringer.
> Maybe he got into some bad drugs,
> my mom offered.
I shook my head no but Jack jumped in and said, This one has
been traveling through dimensions.
> What kind of dementia? my mom asked.
Dimensions, Jack repeated. Other realms.

He was looking in my eyes
and seemed to be reading my thoughts.
Sometimes people go silent like this, he explained. Can't quite put all the pieces together and they are waiting for everything to make sense again. Is that right?

I nodded.

Jack closed his eyes. Now I see the old man, he said, just like the other time. But he's kinda faint. I see two other shapes of something but they're very fuzzy. All I can tell is that they are young, but I can barely make them out. Do you know who they might be?

I didn't want to go there yet.

No, I said out loud. I don't.

Jack opened his eyes. You found your voice, he said. So you had some encounters ... out there. (He spread his hands outward in the air.) And it threw you for a bit. Now you are starting to come back.

I guess you could say that, I said.

My mom was crying now.

Jack said, What do you want to happen next?

I want
my father
home,
I said.

Jack looked at my mom.

She stopped crying
and opened her purse.

She looked at her cell phone,
        hit a programmed number
                and gave it
                to me.

Far Away

It rang more than five times and I thought he wouldn't pick up. It was earlier out there and maybe he was still asleep. Or maybe he was awake and knew who was calling. Maybe he didn't want to talk to his wife or his son. Maybe he was out of minutes.

But then he answered.

                              Hello.

Dad?

                              Jeremy.

JTSBP closed his eyes. I knew he was asking angels or spirits or somebody to help out here.

Hey, Dad, I said,
I was thinking.

                              In that slow, funny way he had,
                              my dad said,
                              Thinking is a good thing.

I was thinking
maybe

                              Maybe what?

Maybe
you could
come home.

                              That's what you were thinking?

Yeah.

                    Oh boy.

Silence on the line.

But something was happening. I could feel it. Like electricity in the room. I felt like a little boy again who missed his father. I wanted to plead with him, beg him if need be.

But I didn't.

                    Oh shit, he said.

Oh shit, what?

                    Oh shit, you won't believe
                    who just came into the room.

Who?

                    Your grandfather.

Old Man.

                    Yep. Haven't seen him
                    in a dog's age.

Why do you think he's there?

                    He says because I need strength.
                    He's giving me
                    some kind of lecture.

He does that a lot these days.

                    He been hanging out with you?

Sometimes.

                    Old Man is smart but
                    he can be a pain
                    in the butt.
                    He can get you in trouble.

Tell me about it, I said.

                    He's telling me
                    I should go home.

I dunno.

Dad.

If I lose you, it's 'cause
I'll be out of minutes.
I gotta pay for both
outgoing and incoming calls.

Dad?

Yeah?

Old Man might really mess with you if you don't do what he
wants. You know what he's like.

Oh, I know that. It's just ...
Silence.

Just what?

I'm embarrassed to say
I don't have any money.

What about the job?

The job was crap. Real crap.
Cleaning up on the oil rigs
and back at the yard.
I quit. Now I'm broke.

I guess my mom was following the conversation.
Guess you didn't have to be psychic to figure out what
was being said on the other end.
She reached into her purse again, fiddled with
her wallet
then started waving her credit card
in the air
like a magic wand.
I'm gonna put Mom on the phone, I said.

He began to say, No, don't do that.

But

I had already handed Mom the phone and Jack was nodding
that he and I should leave the room.

Once we had closed the door behind us, Jack handed me a
stick of chewing gum and said,

Don't worry about anything.
I can already see him on the flight.
He's on the red eye from out West,
seat 11B, it looks like.
He's watching a really silly movie
about cowboys and Indians,
only
the Indians are the good guys
in this one.

Fred the Janitor

School seemed different somehow after that.
And Thomas said hi to me when we passed in the halls.
I said hi back. (It wasn't like we were good buddies, but we weren't enemies. We were neutral.)
No Jimmy, no Jenson, not even Old Man.
When it came time for a pop quiz on French verbs, I had squat.
If I was going to pass the year at all, I'd have to start getting serious about school.
I know,
I know.
Do you hear what this sounds like?

And then Caitlan.
Caitlan still looked pale and unhealthy.
She walked fast everywhere she went
and when I tried to talk to her, she seemed embarrassed.
Can we talk? I'd ask.

                    Not yet.
Two days went by.

                    Not yet. I'm still not ready.
                    Soon.
So I hung back.
Waited.

It was a rainy day.
Buckets of rain.
I arrived at the school soaked.
Caitlan grabbed me
when I walked into the school.

> Now, she said.

Fred was in his closet emptying a bucket of rain water.

> This place has more leaks
> than the *Titanic,* he said
> when Caitlan opened the door.

Hi Fred, she said, can we

> use my office? Sure. I was
> just leaving. Got to save this
> sinking ship.

Fred rolled his bucket and mop noisily
out the door and closed it.
Caitlan locked it from the inside.
We were alone with
the sound of rain on the roof.
We were both wet
and shivering.

> Sorry about avoiding you.

S'okay.

> I needed to get it all sorted out.

You okay now?

> I'm better, but still working on it.
> I showed my mom my arms and hands
> and she took me to a counselor.

I'm working things through.
But you've stopped
  Cutting myself?
  Yes. How stupid was that?
Why did you?
  I wanted to feel the pain.
  It somehow felt good.
  Yeah. I know how that sounds.
(There was a long pause.
We both shivered some more
and then laughed a nervous duet.)
Now what?
  You and me. Can we start over?
Of course.
  No Jenson this time.
(Didn't know what to say to that.)
  He was real.
  To me.
  You know?
To me, too.
I don't really know
how that could be.
  I think that what is real to us
  is what we believe is real.
Maybe that's how everything works.
  After we were up on that hill,
  I didn't know what to think.
You seemed pretty mixed up.
  Who wouldn't be?

I guess.
                    I wasn't sure about you,
                              if you were who
          you appeared to be.
                          I wasn't even sure
              you were   real.
I guess that makes sense.
(I tried to say something
 more but no words came out.
My mind was frozen,
 empty.)
                    What?
I was having a hard time breathing.
I'm here, I said, and then gulped for air.
I'm as real as it gets.
                    I know that now.
I looked deep into her dark eyes now. I suddenly lost my own
nervousness and uncertainty. I could see that she was still
confused, still hurting, still unsteady.
But I saw more than that.
                    What do you see?
I see Caitlan. I see someone who has been hurt.
Someone who is getting stronger.
Someone who will survive.
                    I think I need your help.
I'm good with that.
                    But I don't trust myself.
What do you mean?
                    I can't get too entangled.

Entangled?

Before Jenson, there was someone else
and he hurt me. He said he loved me
but he didn't. It was bad.
And then Jenson.

Yeah, Jenson.

And now you are all I have.

I'll be there for you.

But I need you to just

Just what?

Be my friend.

(Yeah, I'd seen   that one coming.)
I'm good
with that,
I lied.

Thank you.

There was an awkward moment of silence
Then
someone was knocking at the door.

Sorry folks, Fred said. I need my office back.
Got another bucketful of rain.

Photo credit: Daniel Abriel

Interview with Lesley Choyce

Where did the story of Jeremy Stone come from for you?

I wanted to move away from prose for a bit and write a novel in verse form. I wanted it to be accessible yet experimental. I didn't have a specific style in mind or a story but I knew it would concern how individual notions about reality shape the way we experience the world.

I had worked with many Aboriginal students and writers and learned from them about alternate ways of perceiving the world we live in. I knew it would be a gamble on my part to write a novel about a young First Nations teen from a first person point of view. So I put off the challenge until, like so many of my characters, Jeremy Stone arrived one day and his voice was loud and clear. I knew that he was unique and unusual and would lead me into unfamiliar territory. That was just the challenge I wanted.

To be honest, I had no idea where Jeremy or the story would take me and heading off into the unknown was exactly what I wanted. It was my own coming-of-age challenge as a writer to follow Jeremy Stone and allow him to send me off into the unknown.

This is your first verse novel. How does using this form affect the way you approach telling a story?

Once I found the voice, I knew the story would be told sparsely and visually. Every word would have to have an impact and the placement of those words would add texture and meaning. The placement of words dictates a kind of reading rhythm. I had to be aware of how the reader would *see* the words and how they would resonate inside the head.

I think the form made me write more slowly and work with multiple and underlying meanings that don't always present themselves in the faster clip of prose writing. I wanted there to be considerable symbolism but didn't want it to be too heavy-handed. I often didn't realize the emerging patterns of those symbols until I went back to rework the first draft.

Do you think telling this story in verse gives it a more powerful impact than telling it in prose might have done?

I think it presents bigger challenges for readers. My hope was the "poetry" here would not scare readers away. My goal was to weave a complex and challenging tale that would surprise and satisfy true literary readers. But I was also hoping the sparse nature of the text might lure readers who don't like big thick novels but who could be led into the complex, intriguing, paradoxical world of Jeremy Stone's reality.

Jeremy learns a great deal from Old Man, and from the spirits of Jenson Hayes and Jimmy Falcon. The spirit world is

very much a part of Jeremy's life. What interested you in a character who is sensitive to such experiences?

Ah, that is at the heart of the story. Most of us feel we are fairly certain as to what is "real" and what is "not real." If we can see it and hear it, it must be real. We assume thoughts and fantasies are *not* real because they are just inside our minds. Yet we are fully shaped by our beliefs and many of those beliefs are not fully tangible to others. For Jeremy, things of the spirit world are as real as, or more real, than what goes on around him. That is his reality. It is what shapes him and makes him who he is.

Buddhists (and others) would suggest that things on the physical plane of existence are just illusions. The only true reality is experienced when we die and are freed of our bodies so we can perceive the true reality behind the veil of illusions that is our physical world.

Some Mi'kmaq writers I've known speak of the ability to "move between worlds." That includes living in a Mi'kmaq world but also being able to function in the white world. It also allows them to embrace more than one religion: traditional Mi'kmaq beliefs and Christian beliefs together. Truly spiritual individuals also become adept at the bigger challenge of moving between the physical world and the spiritual world. Jeremy has this ability and is able to bridge both worlds on a daily basis, making his life much more interesting and richer than those which most of us experience.

Old Man is an Aboriginal archetype, but Jenson and Jimmy are contemporary young men who have spiritual dimensions. To Jeremy, they are all as real to him as anyone else. This makes for a fascinating character who must realize that most other people don't have his perceptions and his skills. Maybe we all inhabit a world where we are surrounded by individual spirits. Most of us can't see or hear them, but it doesn't mean they aren't there. We're just not trained to notice them or have conversations with them as Jeremy does.

Strangely, as I was writing this book, Jeremy himself was as real to me as any person I was encountering outside the story. Whatever this book, this collection of thoughts, ideas, images, and dialogue was about, there was a "spirit" of some sort that emerged during the creation of the novel. And that spirit, *Jeremy Stone*, became even more tangible as the book progressed. I'd sit down and wonder, *What will Jeremy do next?* Then his quiet, poetic voice in the back of my head would speak and say, "Just wait and see what I have for you."

So, does that make me crazy? Could be. But lucky me. I am no great spiritual guru or visionary like my protagonist but I have the license to be a fiction writer spending part of my day making up the company I keep as I go. And *Jeremy Stone* was a great companion to spend my days with.

E.M. Forster put it thus: *In the creative state, a man is taken out of himself. He lets down a bucket into his subconscious, and draws up something which is normally beyond his reach. He mixes this thing with his normal experiences and out of the mixture he makes a work of art.*

In writing *Jeremy Stone*, I soon realized I was way out of my depth (in that well) and I loved the process immensely as a result.

The intriguing thing is that, while Old Man is the spirit of Jeremy's grandfather, Jenson and Jimmy are spirits of people who never existed in the "real" world. Yet they give Jeremy guidance in that real world. Can you explain that?

This is where I was beginning to experiment with boundaries. What if things of the spirit and of the imagination are very much connected ? And I think they are. I don't have any firm belief system here, but then I'm a fiction writer. As in *Living Outside the Lines*, I can experiment with possibilities. Jimmy was very real to Jeremy. Jenson was very real to Caitlan. Both had profound influences on the living, just as my fictional characters have some strange influence me. Jeremy taught me to keep my mind open to various possibilities of what is real and not real and to respect the personal belief system of others. Of course, once the book is published and I unleash my characters on the unsuspecting public, these fictional "spirits" may have an impact on the thoughts, beliefs and actions of "real" people.

Though Jeremy is a teenager, he is dealing with a lot more than most teens face giving emotional support to his mother and to Caitlan, "reeling" his father home, and helping to change the behavior of Paper Clip. What gives Jeremy his strength?

Jeremy's strength comes from a number of things. He has grown up with a base of powerful spiritual and cultural awareness from an early age. Even though he doesn't fit well into the white world of school and community, he has this extra body of belief and knowledge that helps him survive the everyday difficulties of that world.

He is by nature compassionate and his spirit is kind. He may use angry language, as all kids do when growing up, but his actions are not malevolent or unkind.

Jeremy is also not afraid to be himself. He knows he is different and accepts that as an important part of his identity, so he knows what it's like for others who are different too, especially Caitlan. It also seems that he's been treated very much like an equal, as an adult, by both of his parents, since he was quite young. That, too, has given him an inner strength and greater compassion than the average young man.

You like to tell stories in which not every problem is resolved at the end. Yet some readers like to know that a story is completed in the final page. What do you have to say to those readers?

If I've done my job, a character like Jeremy will seem very real to the reader; maybe just as real as he seems to me. So I like to leave the illusion that life goes on for Jeremy after the last page of the book. And maybe it does on some other level of reality. Usually, there are no tidy endings to the chapters of our own lives. We solve one darn thing only to realize we are up to our eyeballs in the next messy, complicated problem. As the book ends, Jeremy has begun to move on to the next challenging phase of his life and so the story continues on some alternate plane of existence.

You are a person with many diverse interests. You are a singer, a surfer, a poet, a publisher, a teacher, a storyteller. How do all those parts of your life contribute to the stories you choose to tell?

From writing songs, I learned about using words as sounds instead of just visual representations on a page. And I started out my writing career as a poet. My first book was a little volume of poetry called *Re-inventing the Wheel*. I have continued to write poetry as well as novels and, in 2013, published *I'm Alive. I Believe in Everything*, a volume of new and selected poetry written over a forty year period. I have always believed in poetry and loved the possibilities of breaking free of the rules and limitations of standard paragraphs and sentences.

I'm not sure how surfing influences me as a writer, but maybe it goes something like this. Surfing is the art of tapping into those invisible energies travelling through deep waters and matching your energy to theirs as they manifest themselves near the shorelines of continents. It has taught me that when you get smashed by those powerful forces of nature, you take the punishment, surface, get back on your board, paddle out, and try again. Writing novels is often like that.

As a publisher, I worked with Mi'kmaq elder Rita Joe when she was alive to create the first *Mi'kmaq Anthology*, and I admired her quiet, deep, and compassionate spirit. She sent me on a couple of spirit quests including a search for a nearly-lost petroglyph in Bedford, Nova Scotia. I'd like to think her spirit was gently guiding me (or Jeremy) in the creation of this book. I also worked with a number of other gifted Mi'kmaq writers for a second anthology published in 2011.

Certainly as a teacher, I learned many things from my students that went into this book. I teach in the Transition Year Program at Dalhousie University, a program for Black and Aboriginal students. Many of my Mi'kmaq students shared experiences, ideas and beliefs from their culture and traditions. So I was a good listener and I learned a lot. (However, if fall rolls around and I discover I have a student named Jeremy Stone on my class roster, I may be a bit freaked out.)

And finally, as a storyteller, I just know I'd be lost if I had to live only in the so-called real world all the time. I don't exactly "escape" into fiction. I immerse myself in it (like the ocean) when I sit down to write, and grieve when a novel is over, leaving me ever anxious to tell the next story and write the next book. Like everyone else, my lifetime is relatively short. I want to live as many lives as I possibly can in this brief tenure here on the planet.

Thank you, Lesley, for the insights you've provided here.

Lesley Choyce can be found on the internet at:
www.lesleychoyce.com